SILK

In the same universe:

Slay: An Erotic Tale

Coming soon:

Spear: An Erotic Tale

For some queer time-travel adventure…
Check out the Turning Points series
at jodielane.com

The Siege of Masada
Transylvanian Knight
To Kill An Emperor
Renaissance Woman
Heart and Stomach of a Queen

and

The Dark Office
(with Turning Points short stories)

SILK

AN EROTIC TALE BY

MICHELLE MARIPOSA

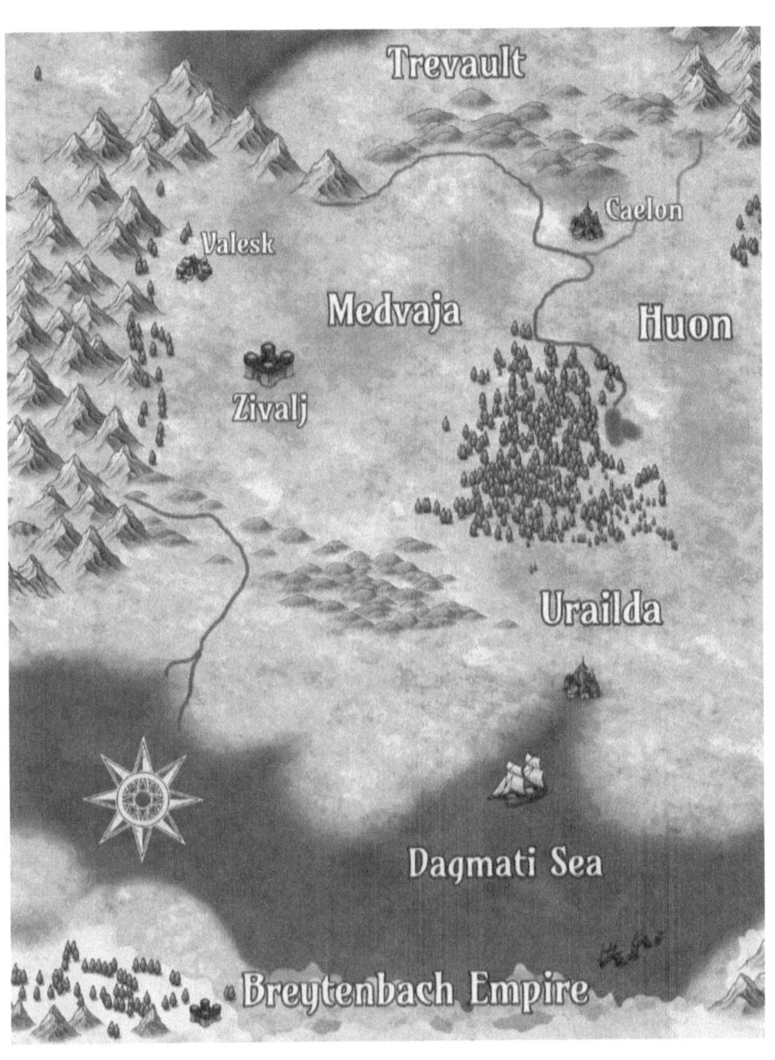

Medvaja and surrounding lands

We must love and mourn in equal parts,
or forever fear a broken heart.

One

I'm a fool for a pretty face and a beckoning smile. Tonight I wonder if my foolishness has gone too far.

"And you actually saw a dragon, Dame Yatina?" Lady Imogen's breathless question makes me smile, though of course my ego attributes it to the fact I'm trailing kisses down her neck.

Yes, the neck of a court lady. A noblewoman. And me, a palace guard. *Have I lost my mind?*

We're tucked into an alcove not far from the entrance of the banquet hall, and I wonder if my senses have truly left me to risk entangling with a noblewoman behind a curtain where anyone could stumble upon us. I know my appetite for danger leads people to call me reckless, but ever since my promotion to Lead Spear, I've been trying to turn that reputation around.

Coming back from the Exchange, or dragon runs, as we guards were calling them, must have triggered something in me, because I let myself be drawn into flirtatious conversation as she clearly hovered in the hallway.

Lady Imogen, with her pale green gown hugging her gorgeous curves, blonde tresses curled around a delicate finger as she lingered in the hallway, making eyes at me. Lady Imogen, her playful banter and admiring smiles, touching my elbow quite overtly, leaning in close and batting pale lashes at me. I followed her quite eagerly as she drifted into this alcove and now I'm breathing in her floral scent, relishing the softness of her skin under my lips, even as I ignore the voice in my head that yells, *This is not a good idea!*

Then she asks about the dragons. I lift my head and answer casually, aiming to impress, "I saw a score of dragons on my tour. But they were mostly juveniles," before returning to my delightful exploration of her exposed collarbone. I must say I'm loving the current fashion of low wide necklines—it suits her large breasts marvelously, and a small part of me pants at the thought of slipping her dress off her shoulders.

"Did you see any… oh! Any adults?"

I grimace. *If I'd known that this was going to be questions about dragons…* After weeks of traversing the western foothills in order to locate the ideal place for the Exchange, then riding escort to the princess as this new, tense agreement played out, I just want to release some of the pent-up stress. I should have gone into the city, to a tavern or a brothel, but as Lead Spear I am expected to make an appearance at banquets. *Be reliable!*

I caress Imogen's flushed cheek. "There were a handful of adults to keep them in check, and those…" I whistle for emphasis. "Those are truly huge. Big enough to fly away with a warhorse in its claws, if it wanted to. But they kept their distance, except the leader who spoke to Her Highness."

"My goodness!" Imogen's lovely brown eyes round. "Weren't you afraid?"

I blink, then inhale the scent of her blonde hair. *Rosewater*, I think. "Fear is there to remind you to pay attention," I murmur, feathering my lips over her collarbone. "But I'd rather pay attention to you right now." I capture Imogen's lips, then grunt in frustration when she pulls away.

"We really must go in," Imogen beams as she smooths her gown, intricate pink roses embroidered on the green sleeves. "Will you come sit with me?"

I agree and offer my arm before her words properly register. *Go in, she said, not go find somewhere more private.* She has me escort her into the banquet hall. The moment we are seated amongst a bevy of her fluttering friends, the questions about dragons return. I'm puzzled but perhaps she doesn't want the others to know she was seducing a mere guard, so play along.

Lords and ladies drift here and there as the drink flows and conversation blooms. A sword-swallower elicits gasps as he performs in the space before the dais, before bowing and giving up the floor to a pair of jugglers.

We sit on one of the long side-tables of the great hall. Normally I'm further down the back with the other royal guards, unless I'm on duty, and I'm feeling oppressed by the wide-eyed, clustering ladies who babble at me. I smile and do my best to be charming, glancing about for something to eat, but it appears the main courses are over.

You would have been here sooner if you hadn't become distracted cleaning your weapons this afternoon.

There's no way to extricate myself without appearing rude, so I submit to the excited queries, retreating often to my wine. I cast an eye about for any platters not yet cleared. My stomach rumbles, so I take another sip.

"I still find it hard to believe they are thinking creatures," one older lady remarks. "But Princess Rhea brokered a treaty with them."

Appreciative murmurs sound and glasses are lifted in toast to the dais, where our beloved future queen sits with her betrothed, Gereon of Huon. Eyes alive with laughter, Rhea touches her husband-to-be's arm and says something that causes him to grin.

Between Prince Gereon stands Lord Liam Cahill. Whatever is going on between the three of them seems to be working, and despite myself, I'm impressed, if not a little envious. Not for the men themselves—Gereon is a prince, high above my station, and Cahill is my captain. I find men as attractive as I do women, but it's a matter of principle and common sense to never sleep with someone in my squad, let alone a superior.

You shouldn't be kissing court ladies either. The thought penetrates my tipsy haze. *You can't just walk away like you normally do—there could be consequences.* I banish it and focus on the dais.

It's not the men I envy, nor Rhea as a woman. But I envy the clear devotion both men hold towards our Princess. It's beyond the fealty due to a prospective monarch. I wonder what it must feel like, to want and love someone like that. To not get bored and distracted and hurt people when you want to move on.

But seeing the way Captain Cahill and Lord Gereon have set aside any conflict in order to be with Rhea… leaves me unsettled. That such a thing is even possible… *Don't be naïve, Yatina. Safer to keep it casual, that way you won't break anyone's heart.*

Lady Imogen's squeak of excitement brings me back to the present. "Look at the dancers!"

Delighted applause ripples through the hall as three female dancers swirl in, silk skirts flowing behind like tails and gauze attached to wrists and elbows to create the semblance of wings. They are meant to be dragons. A clear homage to the kingdom's new friendship.

The dancers leap, twirl and sway in their bright dresses. The black-haired young woman closest to my table flows effortlessly from step to step, glass beads sewn into her cerulean bodice to reflect the bright light of the chandeliers. Sea green skirts and gauze ripple with each spin. I'm mesmerized. She is stunning and skilled and so very alive.

She catches my eye and winks.

The dance ends and the performers curtsey with great flourish. Princess Rhea leads the applause, though I wonder if her highness' smile is somewhat sardonic. Gorgeous and talented though the dancers are, they capture none of the majesty and presence of real dragons. Still, the performance had thoroughly entertained the court, if the comments of Imogen and the others are anything to go by.

"Oh, perhaps we should add wings to our dresses for the royal wedding!"

"What a marvelous idea!"

"Do you think Her Highness would take it amiss? What if she plans on wearing wings with her dress?"

"We must find out," someone declares.

They rise in a flurry and advance on the dais, Lady Imogen in the lead. I barely notice, knocking back the rest of my drink and sidling to a servants' door. All I can think of is the black-haired dancer and her wink.

Down the stairs and into the kitchen, I dodge servants coming and going with dessert trays and carafes of wine. I'm no noble, so while my presence below stairs isn't exactly conventional, everyone is too busy to care.

I figure any entertainment hired from Zivalj will be fed before being sent on their way. Spotting two of the dancers seated at the long table alongside several jugglers and the sword-swallower, I congratulate myself with no small amount of smugness.

As I approach my confidence stutters. The dark-haired dancer is nowhere in sight.

"Can I help you, milady?" one of the jugglers asks. Without his garish hat he lacks much of the presence he'd held during his performance, but his expressive face cocked a thick eyebrow.

"I wanted to offer my regards to the dancers," I declare, my self-assurance re-asserting itself thanks to the wine I imbibed. "I've not seen that style. The court was very impressed."

The blonde and redhead exchange glances and dip their heads in gracious acknowledgement. "Your ladyship is very kind," they murmur.

"Oh, I'm not a lady," I correct. "I'm a guardswoman, a dame. But there were three of you? Where is the third?"

"The wagon is leaving shortly for the city." A lovely voice comes from behind me. "Eat up and we can go."

I follow their gazes over my shoulder, and I turn to see the dark-haired dancer, returning from the passage that leads to the stable yard. Her hair is now tied back sensibly and a blue-gray cloak covers her lovely silks.

The juggler coughs. "This… guardswoman was looking for you, Monique." All eyes swivel to me.

"Can I help you, milady?" Monique the dark-haired dancer asks echoing the juggler. Her clipped vowels hold none of the flirtatious warmth displayed in the dance. A wave of shame crashes over me. I'm a drunk ass coming down here and bothering these performers. I would wallop any soldier in my squad who harassed servants, yet here I am doing the same.

"Just wanted to congratulate you all on your performances," I mumble, clearing my throat. "All of you." I make sure my nod takes in the jugglers and sword-swallower. "No doubt you want to get back to Zivalj and to your beds." Thinking about Monique in bed sends a wave of desire through me, but I firmly crush it and give a stiff bow. "Good night."

Conscious of eyes boring into my back as I stride from kitchen, I clip the corner of a table and swear, mortified. I could not make it back to the barracks fast enough, ridiculously grateful my rank affords me the privilege of not sharing my small room. Shucking my boots and stripping out of my dress uniform, I lie on my bed, glowering at the ceiling.

What is the matter with me tonight? Sure, I'd been tense after coming back from the mountains, but... stealing kisses from noble ladies? Chasing after dancers while drunk?

"Ugh." Ashamed, I palm my face. *Why is it every time I get on a roll with being sensible I throw a stick in the cartwheel?*

Thinking of carts made me wonder if the performers were indeed rolling back down the hill to the city. Does the dark-haired dancer have someone waiting for her back in Zivalj? *Someone that attractive won't be lacking for willing partners. Just look at the idiot of a guardswoman whose clumsy attempts probably have her giggling or disgusted even now.*

I blame the wine and roll over, closing my eyes. *I should drink some water, or I'll have a hell of a headache in the morning.* Instead, my hand drifts between my legs in an effort to make myself relax. I want to press hard and get immediate relief, but I know that will bring no real satisfaction.

I force myself to slow. Gentle strokes through my nightshirt, letting the fabric tease my aching sex. I relax; my mind retreats to fantasy, where I can take what I crave and no one gets hurt.

If it had been somewhere different—a tavern, perhaps. I build up the image of drinking with my squad, of the dancer coming up to me and perching on my lap.

My fingers circle as my pulse quickens.

There would be soft touches and sensuous kisses. I'd stroke her nipples through her dress, feeling them peak just as my own do right now. She'd rise and smile, beckoning me to follow as we take a small room upstairs. On the bed I'd splay her out, then feast between her legs, tasting every drop as I make her cry out again and again.

Pushing past my nightshirt, I dip into my own wetness and slide slick fingers up and down until my mind spasms in pleasure. My shuddering breaths quickly calm, as they always do when I'm alone. I'm not satiated, but the edge is gone.

It's not perfect, but it works well enough, and I sleep.

Two

Ughh, I was right about the headache. I wince as sunlight streams through the shutters. Gritting my teeth, I splash water from the basin onto my face, then guzzle the rest from the pitcher. I'm still aroused, as if taking care of myself last night only stoked the fire rather than taking the edge off.

"Nothing to do but sweat it out." I scowl, then rifle through my clothes chest for a clean set of clothes. *Did I forget to send in my laundry again?* I dig out a clean enough pair of breeches and sleeveless tunic, then grab the pitcher and refill it from the pump in the courtyard, drinking more water.

Eat something. I pluck two apples and a bread roll from the mess. I remind myself to chew slowly, ordering my body to behave as I trudge to the training yards and force myself through stretches and footwork drills. I can smell wine in my sweat and try not to retch. More water, move on to unarmed sequences and then weapons.

By the end I am wrung out, but my head is clearer and my thoughts less lethargic. *Everything makes sense when you're training. Just sweat and hard work.*

"Would have thought you'd skip this morning, like any other sensible person," Captain Cahill observes as I towel sweat from my brow.

"Huh," I agree. "Never said I was sensible."

"Excellent! I need someone foolish enough to agree to a favor." He grins, and I understand why Princess Rhea is in love with her best friend. His solidity hides a good humor that makes him an inspiring captain.

"What do you need?"

Cahill claps me on the shoulder. "I have an order at Schmidt's that needs picking up. It's a wedding gift. I'd get it myself, but I've been ordered to present myself to the palace tailors for fittings." He pulls a face.

"Ah." I smirk. "Better you than me, captain. My dress uniform is already cleaned and pressed." I'd surprised myself getting it done so early.

He shrugs. "Gereon has asked if I'll stand up next to him. It's an honor and I want to look my best, so I'll suffer the fittings."

I peer at him, desperately wanting to ask how they made it work, how no one was jealous or angry or felt left out. Instead I nod and say, "It's paid for, I presume? I'm not coughing up for an ornamental oyster knife. Those things don't come cheap."

Cahill laughs. "It's a pair of darts. All paid for, you know Schmidt's doesn't offer credit. Thanks, al Stauberg, I owe you."

I grumble good-naturedly, as is expected, then take myself off to bathe and change. By the time the tenth bell chimes, I'm trotting out the palace gate on a bay gelding, the city laid out below.

Schmidt's is the best weapon smith in all of Zivalj, and probably all of Medvaja. I ogle the knives on display, the spear heads, the rope darts. A beautiful curved saber hangs on the wall, a small colored ribbon tied to its hilt, indicating the blade was sold. *I'll keep volunteering for the dragon-runs.* The extra pay is well worth it, and no one has been eaten yet.

"Can ah help ye?" A stocky woman stomps out from the door that leads to the workshop, her leather apron protecting a rough homespun shirt and breeches.

"Here to pick up an order for Lord Cahill," I declare, my attention still on the beautiful blades. I face the woman, recognizing Mistress Schmidt.

"Aye." Without further acknowledgement, Mistress Schmidt disappears and then reappears with a linen-wrapped parcel. She places it on the counter with a care that belies her rough hands, unwraps it and checks the contents meticulously.

I lean forward, not daring to breathe on the beautiful steel darts. Razor sharp, they resemble spearheads with forged loops at the base, ready to be knotted onto the rope that would swing them into deadly action.

Princess Rhea favors rope-dart—I'm more of a spear woman myself, but I can still take the head off a straw dummy with a dart at twenty paces, easily.

These darts aren't for practice, though. They're inscribed with a crown between wings, the symbolism clear.

They'll be calling her the dragon queen the day she ascends the throne. I clear my throat. "They're stunning."

"Aye." Mistress Schmidt nods. No vanity, just fact, then re-wraps the gift securely. "Thank Lord Cahill for his business."

"I will," I murmur and tuck the parcel respectfully under my arm. Leaving the smithy I wander up the hill. I have plenty of time before I'm expected back at the palace, and I've stabled my horse under Captain Cahill's account, so it's the perfect opportunity to buy a wedding gift for the princess myself.

But what to get? Left and right I pass shopfronts that display weapons and armor—nothing as good as Schmidt's but even so, out of my price range. My feet take me right at the crossroads and into Jewelers Row, but as I stare at bracelets and rings I hesitate. These aren't the things a soldier should buy for her liege. *Should I go back and look at armor? I could see who gives credit…*

"I'm rubbish at this," I mutter, getting an enquiring look from a passing merchant. "This is why I don't do gifts." *Especially for someone who has everything.*

Is that a spark of jealousy? I shake off the feeling. I don't want Rhea's crown, or men, or responsibilities. Because of her I've risen through the ranks from a grunt to Lead Spear of her personal guard, only one step below Captain Cahill. Maybe that's why I feel lacking, but it's foolish to compare myself to a princess. I'm grateful and honored to serve her. She deserves my fealty, and I should try harder to make sure I deserve the position entrusted to me.

And show my appreciation with a decent wedding gift.

Eyes sliding over the displays without truly seeing, I stomp past sculptors and woodcarvers until my steps take me into a street I rarely visit. Small workshops belonging to intent craftsmen and women turn out odd mechanical contraptions that are new to Medvaja.

The window display of a narrow shopfront catches my eye—behind the small pane of glass, an open box housing a delicately carved wooden dancer in a teal dress rotates to a tinkling tune.

I frown, moving closer for a better look. It's not just that the dancer moves of its own volition, it was that it looks like…

"It's pretty, isn't it?" a voice with a soft Breyten accent asks.

I spin, hand to my dagger. The dancer, Monique, stands before me. She's simply adorned in a plain fawn dress belted with white cord, a blue-grey cloak pushed back over her shoulders, concession to the warm day.

"You!" I glance between Monique and the carved wooden dancer. *Am I going crazy? One evening of sexual frustration and you're seeing her everywhere!*

Monique laughs, and I'm entranced to watch how it lights up her whole face. "I shouldn't tease. It is me, or at least, it's based on me. My uncle made it. Would you like to come in and see it closer?"

A series of inappropriate responses burbles to my lips before I bite them off, the tamest of which is *I'd love to see you a bit closer.* Clearing my throat, "Of course."

Following the dancer, I hesitate once inside. The shop is tiny. I hunch my broad shoulders and tuck my elbows in, a lumbering bull compared to her soft grace.

Wooden clocks and toys and ornaments cover the walls. Some are tiny, little spokes and cogs clicking as pendulums swing back and forth. Others mimic animals, bears pacing in a circle or eagles extending and retracting their wings. The ticking in the otherwise quiet shop reminds me of crickets in the grass, like the fields near my village. For a moment I'm back there, hiding in the barley, avoiding chores. Then Monique gently touches my arm and I snap back.

"Your uncle made all of these?" I ask, then feel as if I've spoken too loudly. I lower my voice. "How do they work? What makes them move?"

"He did, together with my mother." Monique gestures. "They both design and build all sorts of clockwork devices. Do you like them?"

I take in the moving array. *Clockwork.* Gereon mentioned he'd seen it in the Breytenbach Empire, a cold, mountainous land to the south, filled with mysterious mages and ambitious architects.

"I've never seen anything like them. They are… incredible." My eyes fall on the music box in the window. "But that is my favorite. Is it for sale?"

"For sale?" A voice with a much stronger accent comes from the back room. "Which one?" A craftsman emerges, wiping his hands on his apron. "Oh, *ja*, the music box? No, that one is not for sale, I am afraid. I have many others. Can I interest you in one?" He lifts the hinged section of the wooden counter and spots Monique. "Hallo, *liebling*, did you bring lunch?"

The dancer smiles, lifting the basket slung over her arm. "Yes, uncle, I'll take it to mother. Don't let me keep you from talking to a customer." She slips past him and disappears into the back.

I clear my throat. *Might as well get something—they are unique, and I know Rhea likes music.* "I'm after a gift, but I'd like it to be useful as well as pretty."

Monique's uncle nods, his movements deft as he reaches up to a shelf hosting a display of carved boxes. "Of course, of course—utility has its own beauty, my creations aren't just to delight the senses. Does the recipient keep the trinkets, or need a place to store the jewelry?"

"Jewelry," I reply confidently. Even if she doesn't wear an excessive amount, the princess certainly owns it.

"Mm, *ja*, very good, very good." He twists the key inserted into the back of the box, then opens the lid. A bluebird flaps and bobs, its beak opening and closing as music played.

"Do you have something larger?" *Maybe I should ask how much before committing.* But I'm sure Rhea doesn't have anything like this. Besides, the longer I take, the more chance Monique will come back out... *Sweet ancient gods, Yatina, you have a problem!*

To distract myself I try to remember what kind of ornaments or jewelry I've seen in the princess' chambers. A memory flashes of the last time I'd been in there—Rhea drinking mint tea in a silk dressing gown, hair still mussed. Gereon and Liam eating breakfast, joking about something while I waited to report on the status of the northern border forts. Envy and arousal stir in me again—not for any of the nobles, but for the easy companionship they seem to share.

Monique's uncle presents several more options before I settle on a large music box of beechwood, a wheel of dolphins rotating to a lilting tune. I've never actually seen a dolphin, but Monique's uncle assures me the depiction is most accurate, as he hails from the south. *Explains the accent.*

"My sister and I, we grew up by the seashore—we often saw the dolphins and the whales and even the great sea serpents. We made the apprenticeship together and do our best to bring the marvels of nature into our work."

"Your sister?" Monique had mentioned her mother.

"*Ja*, Leticia loves to create the clocks with the birds. Gulls, hawks, nightingales. These are her work."

"What is your name, sir?" I ask as he excitedly showcases the wall of mechanical timekeepers, adorned with carvings of birds.

"Me? Olaf Yulic. Please mention my name, and that of my sister, to your friends, good lady. We are new to Medvaja, and our little creations are still a novelty here in Zivalj, but I hope they shall—how do you say—catch on."

Digging out silver pieces, I consider the contraptions and carvings. "You might think about dragons," I suggest as Olaf fussed over wrapping her purchase. "They are very popular at the moment."

His hands still. "I have never seen a dragon. I would not know where to start."

"I could describe one to you." Part of me is reluctant to become the target of another barrage of questions, but he doesn't take my meaning.

"Hmm, a picture would be best," he says absently. "I'll think on it. Thank you, good lady."

I linger a few moments longer, then feel foolish. I'm keeping him from his lunch, so I bow my thanks and step out.

Three

Outside the shop, cradling both gifts carefully, I pause to shelve my disappointment. "You're in a real mood today, aren't you soldier?" I mutter. *I'll make sure I'm on the next dragon run.* Hard training and the chill autumn air of the foothills would cure me of this mood. Maybe after a visit to the Street of Flowers.

"I never caught your name, Lady…?" Monique's voice behind me sends my focus into a spin.

I cough, trying not to blush at my previous thought. "Ah, Yatina. Yatina al Stauberg. Lead Spear of the Royal Guard under Lord Cahill. I'm not a lady."

Monique's eyebrows raise. "An impressive title, Yatina al Stauberg, Lead Spear."

I frown. Is she teasing me? "And you are Monique… Yulic? Or that is just your uncle's name?"

Monique nods solemnly, then a smile curls one corner of her lips. "Yulic is also my name, and my mother's. We are newly come to Medvaja. I see you found something to your liking?" She indicates the wrapped jewelry box.

"A gift." *Ugh, why I am being awkward?* For all that I avoid court ladies, I don't normally have a problem talking to pretty women! And Monique is pretty. Beautiful, even. She holds herself gracefully, as a dancer should. Shoulders back, movements fluid. Her long black hair curls around her slim neck in a thick plait, and the way she speaks her vowels at the front of her mouth has me transfixed.

"For your lover?" Monique's dark brown eyes sparkle. "You are very generous."

"No!" I shoot back, wincing at how abrupt I sound. I clear my throat. "No, it is for the princess. A wedding gift."

Now it's Monique's turn to look surprised. "You are friends with the princess?" A look of trepidation crosses her face. "I meant no insult."

"I've served her many years," I explain. "We've fought together, and that forms its own kind of bond."

Monique raises her eyebrows.

"Not that kind of bond!" Defensiveness spikes. There is no way I am going to discuss my future monarch's preferences to this stranger, no matter how pretty and charming.

"I did not mean to imply anything untoward," the dancer apologizes. "Forgive me."

An awkward silence hangs between us, then Monique ventures, "So… you liked the dancing last night?"

Warmth starts in my belly and creeps up to my face. *I liked watching you dance. I like listening to you talk too.* "It was most… enchanting."

Monique nods thoughtfully. "You liked it so much you wanted to tell us straight after the performance. You wanted to tell me, the others said."

The blush rises in full now, but I manage to straighten my shoulders. "I apologize for my behavior last night. If anyone in the palace, noble or otherwise, ever approaches you while you are there, you are not obliged to return their favor. It is most unacceptable. I was in my cups, but that's no excuse."

Monique stares at me, then understanding dawns. "Oh! Is that why you are so stiff and awkward speaking to me today? I thought perhaps you weren't comfortable speaking to women and regretted trying to find me last night."

I blink. "I am not stiff! Nor am I awkward," I declare, trying to ignore the rigidity of my back, a perfect parade stance. "I have no trouble speaking to women, I just regret the manner in which I approached you. It was most uncouth."

She laughs, a delighted sound. "You are so very stiff, and formal too. Uncle could make a perfect clockwork soldier modeled on you, it's wonderful."

I go to retort, then stop. Perhaps I should feel insulted, but... there's no malice in Monique's words. I take a deep breath and relax, dropping into the casual stance of a soldier about the town, implying swagger even when still. "Sweetheart," I drawl. "That clockwork soldier couldn't do half the things I can do." I look Monique up and down meaningfully.

She shouts with laughter, and I grin. Leaning forward, I breathe in the dancer's scent of fresh cut wood and sunshine. "If you'd like to take a stroll with me sometime, perhaps I could buy you a drink?"

Monique doesn't retreat, though she seems to hold her breath. Then her dark eyes look up at me and a sensual smile crosses those lovely, full lips. "I'll be at the palace dancing again tonight. Are there any rules about seeking you out?"

I tense. "None at all."

She lifts a hand as if to touch my face, then draws back thoughtfully. "Perhaps I'll see you." She smiles and drifts back into the shop.

I gaze after her, then at the music box dancer still twirling slowly in the window, then palm my forehead. *Such a fool for a pretty smile.* But I can't deny the excitement that bubbles in me, and I know I need to find out what happens next.

"You seem in a much better mood, al Stauberg," Captain Cahill comments when I deliver the parcel from Schmidt's.

I reply blithely, "Fresh air does wonders for the soul." I keep imagining what it would feel like to kiss Monique, to trail fingers along her olive skin. More than once a distracted shiver runs through me, and I fight to concentrate on duty rosters, inspections and briefing the volunteers who are to accompany me on the next Dragon Run, which is happening much sooner than I expected.

"This time you're going to go without me," Princess Rhea advises as we finish inspecting the squad who are to go. "You'll be back in time for the wedding, but I can't afford to be away from the palace with all these dignitaries arriving. Kyan will assign a liaison to you."

It gives me a strange tremor to hear her talk about a dragon in such a casual manner, as if Kyan is a visiting cousin, rather than a huge, scaled beast with dark green wings and claws that could disembowel a horse. During the first Exchange, I had been ordered to hang back and stand guard on the frightened, if well-paid, herders, while Captain Liam and Princess Rhea had strolled up to the gigantic creature to discuss the feeding arrangements for the clutch of baby dragons. I'd fought the instinct to attack or flee, but it bubbled just under the surface as the wyrms gorged themselves on the herd of fat sheep in the steep valley before falling asleep.

The adults didn't join in the feasting, which was just as well because the sheep barely fed the juveniles. *What would happen if they decided they were hungry, too?*

I hide my trepidation. "Of course, Your Highness." *I won't let you down.*

"Excellent. You'll be meeting the cowherds at Valesk, day after tomorrow, and escort them from there."

I salute. Rhea dismisses me with a smile and I return to the barracks to ready myself for the banquet.

I slip in late, keen to avoid Lady Imogen, eating with members of my squad. Avoiding the wine, I loiter without chatting as various entertainers perform. Jugglers, acrobats, singers, and, of course, the dancers.

This time Monique is paired with an athletic young man. He lifts and spins her, her grace seemingly effortless as her gauzes float in her wake. I become absorbed in the joy of watching her, her dazzling smile as she dances several sets. The troupe is larger than the previous evening, but none of her partners, male or female, hold a candle to her.

One part of the dance involves bounding gracefully into the surrounding audience, scattering petals from baskets.

I'm not entirely surprised but still quite delighted when Monique twirls in front of our table, bestowing fresh rose petals upon the other guardsmen and women and me. Quick as a bird, the dancer plucks a tightly folded circle of parchment from her cleavage and flings it into my lap, so smoothly and swiftly it looks like just another petal. The rigidity of the parchment, however, is nothing like the silky petals, and I clutch it, keeping my smile plastered, hoping none of the others notice as they clap and Monique moves on.

When their performance ends and the whole hall resounds with applause, Monique glances my way and blows a subtle kiss. I tense, hungry in the most physical way. I fake a yawn and stroll from the table, attempting to appear unhurried.

Unfolded, the note reads, *Western Fountain. Eleven bells.*

My chest tightens and my thighs warm. It seems fairly clear on the surface, but I don't want another Lady Imogen situation where clearly I misinterpreted her interest. Shooting a wary look in the half-empty hallways around me, I am relieved no noble ladies stand there to accost me. *Definitely dodged that arrow. Hopefully she just forgets and moves on.*

Monique seems a surer wager, and evidently I've redeemed myself after my drunken bumbling of the previous night.

But it's not very… sensible. I hadn't been thinking when I'd kissed Lady Imogen, merely flattered and excited. Was I thinking now? I swallow, my mouth dry, and observe that I've started walking despite myself, aiming for the gardens on the western side of the palace.

It's harmless. Just a quick rendezvous, then back to being responsible. It won't happen again.

~ | ~

The stars are out in force. Not as many as grace the wild night skies of the western foothills, with no lamps and torches on every corner to chase away the empty, rolling darkness. But a glittering array still scatter the heavens above me, waiting for the moon to rise.

A soft breeze plays through the gardens as I scope the fountain, keeping to the shadows, my senses on alert.

How long does it take to make her excuses? Or has she changed her mind? Perhaps eleven bells have already rung and I'd not noticed.

The dull ache of desire builds within me to the point of discomfort and I shift. If the dancer doesn't show, I'm not sure I can just go to bed tonight. I'll have to ride into the city and find a tavern, or even just go straight to the Street of Flowers. *Where's your discipline, soldier?* A scornful voice asks. *Some captain you'll make if you can't even keep your breeches on.*

My trail of thought is broken as the sonorous toll of the bell begins and a figure enters the courtyard, moving lightly under its voluminous cloak. It stops by the fountain, looking around. The relief that fills me assuages my desire for a moment, then the burning need returns.

"You dance beautifully," I say, my voice husky. I step forth from the hedgerow, a small part of my brain thinking it would be ironic if the cloaked figure isn't Monique, but some other person seeking a romance. What lie would I tell then?

The figure throws back its hood, revealing dark hair and a seductive smile. "Why, thank you." Monique curtsies.

As I reach her my worries fall away. The prickle of cinnamon hair oil fills the air, tingling the senses. Standing very close, I gaze down and long for better light so I can decide where to start unpinning that beautiful hair. The thought of seeing it mussed out on my bed sends my stomach into a spin.

I compel myself to savor the darkness instead, lifting a hand to cup Monique's face, leaning down slowly and brushing those soft lips. A rush of sparks flow from between my thighs to my breasts.

I close my eyes, relishing the buildup, the tantalizing crest of the wave before it crashes. My hands run up Monique's side, aching to squeeze, to grip, to feel, but I force myself to caress.

"Hmm." Monique melds into me. Heat blooms. The dancer entangles her fingers in my short hair, pulling me down and kissing me ardently.

Oh, yes. She is most definitely interested.

Excitement threatens to overwhelm me. My breath races as my hands tremble across every enticing curve, every plane within reach. Her physique is firm without being hard, not heavily muscled like me, but wonderfully strong beneath her gown.

We should really move away from the fountain, into the darkness of the hedgerow. An intelligent person would. An intelligent person wouldn't be out here in the first place, risking their rank and reputation for a… for a…

Sweet ancient gods, save me. "You smell so good," I murmur, common sense fleeing like a coward from a battlefield as I inch the fabric of Monique's skirt up and touch soft skin. Her soft panting as I trail my fingers higher up her thigh threaten to make me lose control.

Holding my arm firmly across the dancer's back, I use my knee to nudge one of Monique's legs up onto the fountain edge and let my fingers tease closer to that warm and intoxicating center.

"Ohh," Monique moans. I kiss her quiet. I want the stars above to be the only witnesses. This is stupid, this is public, yet I cannot stop. All I can think about is that I will die if I don't get to taste her. I need it.

As my fingers sweep higher, Monique shudders and cries out. I swallow the sound with my mouth as the dancer's foot slips and goes straight into the fountain.

Four

"Oh!"

"Shit!" I curse as I stagger, my weight all wrong. Twisting to pull the dancer clear, I fall sideways, landing in the fountain on my ass.

"Cock-sucking, pox-ridden, whoreson idiot!" I spit. Monique's face is contorting like she's having a fit, and I realize I'm glaring. I cast my eyes down. "I'm sorry, that wasn't at you."

"Are you alright?" Monique clutches one hand to her mouth. She's trying not to laugh.

"What's going on out there?" a deep voice demands.

"Oh shit." Mortified, I sweep wet hands through my hair and clamber out of the fountain. *This is what you get for making stupid choices!* I glower at the surrounding garden, daring anybody hiding behind the topiaried trees to cackle.

A heavy-set man steps out from the arbor to my right. It's Brayton Greyvensteyn, captain of the king's royal guard, stern as he is dedicated to King Denusake's safety. "Al Stauberg?" he frowns at me, then slides suspicious eyes to Monique.

I clear my throat. "Tripped and fell in fountain, sir,"

His eyebrows snap together. "Not usually so clumsy, are you." It's not a question, and I can't deny it. He's seen me train.

"I bumped her, I'm sorry, sir," Monique pipes up.

He runs his eyes over her, not in a rakish way, simply assessing whether she stands as a threat. "You're one of the dancers from this evening." He really misses nothing. "What are you doing out here?"

"I expressed a desire to see the gardens, and Dame al Stauberg was kind enough to offer me a tour." She beams at him.

He isn't fooled, giving her a stern look. "Bit dark for that. Best you get back to your group before the wagon leaves for the city." He's letting us off lightly, not asking embarrassing questions which I'd be hard-pressed to answer. I can't lie to save my life.

"Yes, sir." I salute. "Thank you, sir."

He nods, his eyes missing nothing as Monique and I pass, carefully maintaining a respectable distance. "Oh, al Stauberg," he adds, "her highness has been speaking very highly of you to the king." *Don't make her regret it with your stupid decisions,* is the unspoken reproof.

"I am grateful for that, sir." I hope the darkness hides my flush of embarrassment.

We walk quickly along pathways around the palace, back towards the main gate. I'm silent, but Monique is trembling. She's still trying not to laugh. Anger rises, but she speaks.

"That's not—" Monique tries again. "That's not what I had in mind when I wanted to get you—get you wet!" Tears stream down her face as her eyes crinkle with mirth.

Something loosens within, even as I drip with water and indignation. My pride relents. "I thought I was doing quite well until that moment." My comment is far drier than the rest of me.

Monique clasps my hands. "But you are not hurt?" She gazes up, genuinely caring, if still smiling. "No, you seem quite fine. I'm so sorry, my ankle tweaked at the exact wrong angle and I lost balance."

I straighten, feeling like the clockwork soldier she named me. "It would take more than a tumble into shallow pool to injure me," I declaim. Then I relax a fraction. "My dignity is the only thing to have taken a beating."

"Not at all." Monique kisses me, taking me by surprise. "You are still most dignified."

Warmth flows through me. "Will you be dancing here again tomorrow night?" I ask. I have to see her again.

She shakes her head. "Not tomorrow. I'll be at the Silver Fawn, my usual for the rest of this week." She smiles at me, half shyly, half hopeful. "You're welcome to come and watch?"

The words are out of my mouth before I even think. "I'll be there."

~ | ~

The Silver Fawn is a semi-respectable establishment, half dance-hall, half tavern, where one can get sloshed while trying to impress your guy or girl with discerning comments on the quality of the entertainers. The wine isn't bad, the ale better, and the bowl of sunflower seeds gives me something to do with my hands while I keep an eye on both stage and room.

"The Breytenbach girl? Should be on in a few more sets," the barmaid tells me as she serves my drink, wipes a spill expertly before swooping away to clear tables.

I'm expecting something like the dancing at the palace for Monique's act, but when she saunters into view, I blink hard. Gone are the ethereal silks and flourishes. No gauze floats behind. She wears a tight-fitting dress with splits all the way up to her thigh, shoes with a hard heel that clip-clops on the wooden boards. Patrons whistle and clap as she throws an alluring smile over one shoulder, then taps her foot as a drum beat begins.

Her hips begin to sway, then her arm shoots out in time with the blast of a brass horn. Deliberate steps and bold movements accompany the rhythm—I am entranced, forgetting my ale, the sunflower seeds, the other people clapping and hooting encouragement with each high kick, each sharp spin. She dominates the room, the music building as her dance becomes more dramatic, more intense.

She finishes with a spectacular spin and sinks into the splits, arms raised in triumph. I'm clapping like an idiot with the rest, but unlike them, I don't return to my drink and conversation as we wait for the next act. I stare at the slightly tattered curtain as she disappears behind it. *Should I go backstage and find her?*

There is no need. From a side door, Monique appears, still in her figure-hugging dress. She smiles straight at me, says something to a barmaid then wends her way between tables. A pair of Uraidlan singers have started their performance, but a few members of the audience notice Monique and offer their compliments as she passes. She smiles graciously and nods her thanks until a short man with a tattoo on his neck stands up and halts her progress.

"Can I buy you a drink? Me and the lads wanted to pay our compliments to such a lovely dancer." He leers a little. I immediately tense. The three other men sitting with him also sport tattoos that mark them as Wyverns, a gang that lurks in the poorer parts of the city.

The smile leaves Monique's face as she takes them in. "Not interested," she says flatly. "Please excuse me, I'm meeting a friend."

The man follows her gaze to where I sit, coiled and ready to leap up. He assesses me, a slight sneer as he sees the patch with the royal coat of arms on my jacket. But then his face turns courteous as he bows to Monique. "Don't let us keep you then."

She slides past, sinking onto the stool next to mine. The barmaid delivers a cup and pours ale, raising her eyebrow to me.

"I'm good, thank you." I hold my hand over my still half-full mug.

"Not drinking?" Monique asks, taking a deep draft, sighing in satisfaction.

"Someone like me needs to keep my wits in a place like this," I answer carefully, sipping, keeping one eye on the Wyvern lads.

Her face falls.

"I doubt they'll cause trouble," I reassure her. "I'd just rather not find out the hard way.

She nods tersely and finishes her ale. "I only have one set tonight. We can leave if you like?"

Surprised, I rise when she does, abandoning my unfinished drink. "And go…?"

Her face transforms back into cheeky flirtation. "You could walk me home. Come with me while I fetch my cloak and change my shoes."

I can't resist that smile. She uses it several more times as I trail through passages and up narrow stairs to a tiny dressing room that holds a rack of costumes, a dresser and a solid wooden chair.

"Oh good, no one else is here." She throws me a sultry look as she lights the bracket of candles on the dresser.

I step close, closing the door behind me with a *click*.

"Is anyone likely to come in?" I murmur.

"Not for a little while at least," she breathes.

In a heartbeat, I spin Monique around and press her back against the door, pinning wrists above her head. I lean in.

"I've been thinking about you all day," I murmur against her ear, feeling her breath catch.

"All day? Surely you had more important things to do." The teasing tone doesn't quite hide the tremor in her voice.

"Mmm." I feather my lips down her jawline, biting ever so gently. "I could barely sleep last night, I wanted you so badly." I repeat the pattern up the other side of Monique's neck, then inhale her tightly braided hair.

Monique wiggles. "I smell like sweat from dancing."

"You smell like a treat waiting to be devoured," I growl, then kiss her, crushing her lips fervently with my own, my tongue seeking hers. I press my body against her and drop my hands to caress everywhere I can reach, craving that firm pliancy again. "You feel wonderful."

Breathlessly, Monique asks, "Are you planning on keeping me at the door all night?"

I pull back and give her a demon's grin. I grip her ass and hoist her easily, walking us to the chair and lowering her with care. I kneel before her.

Monique's cheeks are flushed, her eyes bright. I want to unbind that braid, run my fingers through her lovely hair. I want to kiss her soft lips until they are swollen, run my teeth along her collarbone and free her breasts from their bodice. I want to pounce.

But I remove her shoes instead, intending on kissing my way up her long legs. A sigh of pleasure escapes Monique. I cock my head. She flutters her eyelashes.

"It's nice to be off my feet after dancing all evening."

"Oh, trust me, I plan to keep you off your feet." I give one sole a squeeze to emphasize, and almost drop it when she groans.

"Don't stop! That feels wonderful."

Encouraged, I press my thumbs in and circle, intrigued by the sounds of pleasure each movement entails. It's not that I haven't massaged lovers before, it was just I've never encountered such an enthusiastic response. Her eyes flutter closed and her back arches as I work my way up ankles and calves. I wish I had some sort of oil to make my movements smoother, then the vision of her naked as I massage oil into her skin almost has me panting. I force myself not to rush, fascinated by the way she arches and gives quiet, breathy moans.

"Oh, yes, please, that's wonderful, yes." A litany of affirmation starts as I return to the feet, concentrating on one at a time. I work tendons and circle the small muscles, until Monique jerks violently, giving a cry that sounds like agonized joy. She subsides with a lazy, contented chuckle.

Slowly, I take her hands. She smiles at me with half-lidded eyes.

"Did you just…? From me massaging your feet?" I'm perplexed, but holding onto the excitement that that was exactly what had just happened.

Monique blushes and nods. "It was wonderful."

My jaw drops. "Do you normally do that?"

The dancer shrugs. "It's not necessarily my feet. It could be anywhere, depending on my mood."

I prop my head on my fist and inhale her aroma. Our body heat in this tiny room isn't the only thing that has us warm. "That is unheard of. What happens when someone actually…?" I kiss her thigh, keeping eye contact.

"Actually what?" A playful smile and instantly I want to smother those curving lips with my own.

"Actually… makes love to you?" I kiss again, a little higher up. "Even if it's just a quick roll?"

Monique laughs gently, a beautiful sound that tingles through me. "How is what we just did not love-making?

I blink, not knowing how to answer. I know I'm just a soldier, but I still don't want her to think me crass.

She lifts my chin with a finger. "Every touch, every word, can be lovemaking, if you want it to be," she breathes. She leans down to kiss me, then takes my wrists and plays her fingers over helpless palms. "Such strong hands," she murmurs, exploring. "Do they ever get attention, or is it always work, work, work?"

Monique lifts one of my hands and kisses it, then bites gently on the side, where the thumb meets the palm. She kisses and bites again, harder, sending a flurry of sensation through me.

"These hands… are quite good… at what they do." I try to reassert myself. "I can show you."

Monique bites my wrist, and I lurch back in a sitting position. She follows me and straddles my lap, kissing me fiercely. I let my hands roam freely, caressing every curve, shoving the skirt of her dress up.

"Oh, yes," the dancer breathes, as my fingers roam closer and closer and at last brush against the damp heat I'd come so close to last night. I stroke gently, feeling her quiver, gliding through the warm wetness and circling at the top. I withdraw my hand and taste, then return as Monique trembles on my lap. When I slip a finger inside, she moans in the most gratifying way and rocks herself, head flung back wantonly as she closes her eyes and works herself to ecstasy again. I yank the neck of her dress down, capturing a nipple in my mouth I suck hungrily, my control fraying as I curl a second finger inside, gripping onto her waist to keep her in place.

Beautiful. The world shrinks to the two of us. Monique cries out even louder and shudders so violently I panic a moment that she's having a fit. In a boneless heap, the dancer collapses and hums, satisfaction and joy rolling off her in waves. I cradle her as she lolls in my lap.

"Mmm." The dancer nuzzles my neck.

I'm astonished. I've never been with a woman who comes so fast and hard.

Monique chuckles, then mock-glares. "But you interrupted me…" With surprising strength and agility for someone who's just melted into a puddle of sexual bliss, she pushes me backwards onto the floor and tugs off my boots, then my breeches. Surprised, I let myself be divested of the offending garments, then tense as Monique lowers her mouth.

It's not that I don't like the feeling, I just find it easier to give rather than take. It's hard for me to relax at first as she nuzzles my thighs, then kisses, then laps gently at me.

I close my eyes, caressing her hair, now coming loose from its braid. I touch her shoulders, her arms, wherever I can reach.

My hips begin to rock of their own volition. I want to grind myself into Monique's tongue, grab the back of her head and feel our lips mesh. But I hold back, silently begging Monique to kiss, lick, suck harder. The wave rises in my body and mind.

It's so much! It's too much!

I entwine my fingers into her hair and pull hard. She groans and plunges her tongue in deep, then returns it to my peak. Tremors crash through me, waves pounding the shore before slowly subsiding. I shudder and tremble, helplessly caressing Monique's now fully mussed up braid. She crawls up beside me with a smug grin, the both of us lying on the dressing room floor like a youth and a maiden swiving in the barn.

I pull her close, embarrassed, and kiss her, tasting myself. "That wasn't quite what I expected," I say, self-conscious.

Monique shrugs, breasts still exposed, dress still rucked around her waist like a prostitute. I quite like prostitutes and think the look most becoming, but am sensible enough not to say so in case she doesn't share the opinion.

"Predictability is overrated." Monique stifles a yawn.

This startles a laugh from me. "So true," I grin. "Now, I shall walk you home."

Respectably attired, we sneak out of the Silver Fawn and walk the cobbled streets, thinning fast of evening traffic as people hurry home. I'm glad the artisans district has well-tended lamps every few dozen yards.

"Will I see you again?" I ask abruptly as we reach the clockwork shop. *Since when do you see people again?*

That tantalizing smile again. "If you like."

I tingle all over.

We reach the door and I bow, kissing Monique's hand, strangely desirous of giving her formal courtesy. Her amused smile stays with me as I walk back to the stable where I left my horse, and ride up the hill to the palace. I fall asleep, lulled by the scent of the other woman still clinging to my skin.

Five

Despite the late night, I wake energized. I relish the smell of sweat and the ache of the morning's training. The simplicity reassures me; acting and reacting, not thinking. *Thrust, parry, strike, block.*

I grunt as I disarm an opponent, holding the blunted end of a practice spear to their throat.

"Nicely done," Anasta, my sparring partner, grins and steps back. I salute her in return.

"You made me work for it," I declare.

She shakes her head. "You're a demon with a polearm, Yatina. Show me how you got past my block."

In the afternoon, I brief the soldiers who will accompany me back to the western foothills. Six of them would form the squad, including Anasta. It's a reduced number after the first dragon run went so well. Personally, I feel twenty or even thirty soldiers wouldn't go amiss—we are dealing with dragons, after all. But Rhea had stipulated that a smaller squad would move lighter and faster, and our main job is to stop the herders from wandering off and getting eaten.

"The adult dragons are your main protection," Rhea assures me. I hope the princess' trust in these creatures isn't misplaced.

I had forgotten to tell Monique I would be gone at least a week, so I scrawl a brief note and pay a pagegirl half a silver to run it into the city, care of the clockwork shop. Not that I want to give the dancer ideas. But I definitely want to see her again, and that puts me in a good mood. not to mention leaving before dawn gives me an excellent excuse to skip the banquet, so I don't run the risk of being ensnared by Lady Imogen again.

I pack my saddlebags and go to bed early. By the time the sun rises, peeking through soft pink clouds, we are on the road to Valesk. The village is one of the furthest west in the realm, and makes an ideal mustering point for this… tribute? Trade? I don't quite know what to call it. Yes, I know officially it's called the Exchange, according to the treaty Princess Rhea brokered with Kyan of the Malachite clan. It makes it sound less subservient, but I don't really see anything coming back our way.

Have some cows and sheep and please don't raid our villages. Sounds like a protection racket to me, though I must admit that with King Thetin of Trevault threatening war on the northern border we need soldiers there, not protecting villagers' flocks from voracious baby wyrms.

But what stops the dragons deciding they want a bigger meal? Have we gotten into bed with an enemy? The alliance with Huon will only take us so far.

I sigh and focus on the western mountains as my bay clops patiently along. Yesterday I had been full of satisfaction and purpose. *Where are all these gloomy thoughts coming from?*

A pleasant distraction comes in the shape of one of the herders who meets us in the late afternoon on the outskirts of Valesk. Rafe is handsome and has the tan and long stride of someone who spends their life outdoors.

"The cows are in the paddock over there. Thirty head." He speaks unhurriedly. "We'll be ready t'leave at dawn." The other herder, a whey-faced girl with lank hair, nods shyly.

~ | ~

"You don't seem bothered by the prospect of dragons?" I ask him the next morning as we climb the trail into the first of many valleys that grace our route. We've left our horses in Valesk—infant dragons won't bother to distinguish between four-legged meals, so it's safer to stay on foot.

Rafe shrugs, shooting an easy smile as we trudge along the right flank of the herd. Occasionally a cow tries to venture after tastier grass and we shoo it back into line. "Tis gold my family needs. Pirates came up the river from the coast last winter. I was late to bring the herd in, but they took what they could and burned much else besides. Family hid, but we need to rebuild."

I grunt, empathizing. With so many soldiers gone north, are there enough in the river lands? Pirates would strike again if they thought Medvajan forces were diverted. I determine to raise it with Captain Cahill.

Rafe winks at me, displacing my grim thoughts. "Besides, tisn't every day a simple cowherd like me gets to march with the King's soldiers and see dragons."

I throw an approving nod his way. He smiles, and for some reason it buoys my mood.

When we crest the final saddle that drops into the small, narrow valley that is our destination, I tell him, "We'll leave the herd here, but I've got to climb higher and speak to whichever creat– whichever dragon is in charge. You're welcome to join me." I try to sound braver than I feel. Not that I'm trying to impress him, of course not. I just figure if he really wants to see dragons up close, this is his chance.

Rafe nods and whistles to his offsider further back in the line. "Keep 'em coming. Water them at the spring—the dame and I will go t'meet the dragons."

The girl looks relieved that she hasn't been invited. "Are they coming straight here?" she asks, raising her voice over the excited moos—the beasts in the lead scented fresh water.

I understand her fear. I'd been in her position only a few weeks ago. But the princess is trusting me to ensure this Exchange goes smoothly, so I keep an outward face of calm.

"We made good time, I don't expect them to arrive until closer to sundown. Once the cows are all in the valley, you will assemble up on that knoll." I point. The hillock protrudes from the southern side of the slope. "No dragon will enter the valley until we are safely removed from the area. Stay with my soldiers, do not worry if the animals venture further up, only stop them from going back down the trail."

I've drilled my squad in what to expect, to protect the cowherds and stop them running away in panic, but it didn't hurt to repeat it. *Ancient gods know I wanted to run away myself last time.*

I wait until the majority of the beasts are near the stream, then hike with Rafe to the top of a steep incline that borders the valley to the north.

"We'll wait here," I tell him, settling down on the grass and enjoying the cold breeze that scurries down from the peaks, cooling my sweat.

"D'ye not summon them?" he asks, stretching out beside me, closing his eyes, the picture of unconcern.

"Ha!" I consider. "Actually, I don't see why a horn couldn't be used, to let them know we are here." *Not sure I'm brave enough to ask right now.* I distract myself by admiring his tanned frame, then I think of Monique with a jolt. What is the dancer doing right now? Would she be impressed with my duties, or become obsessed with asking dragon questions like Lady Imogen?

A shadow drags me back into the present with a sharp jolt. The boom of giant, leathery wings has me snapping upright and gripping the looped rope-dart at my waist. Barely aware of Rafe scrambling to his feet, my whole focus is on the huge creature landing before me, vermillion scales flashing in the late afternoon sunlight.

Attack! Run! It takes everything I have to stay still. I'd been grateful for Rafe's company before but now I simply pray I won't faint or soil myself in front of him.

The dragon flares its wings for balance before folding them along its back. It peers down its long snout and asks in a voice that purrs like the wind through tall trees, "You are the human sent by Princess Rhea?"

I swallow, dredging up my voice from the pit of my stomach where it seems to have fled. The thing is just so damn *huge*. I've fought smaller wyrms, and, as I'd told Lady Imogen, seen the adults from a distance, but to stand face on when it was less than twenty feet away… *Time to talk, you dolt!*

"I am Yatina al Stauberg, Lead Spear of the Princess' personal guard," I announce, bowing, praying my voice doesn't squeak. I clear my throat. "We have the herd in the valley. I just need time to clear my soldiers and the herders and you may bring your younglings in to feed." *Back straight, you're not a coward, set an example.*

The dragon sniffs, then bends its head in a bow. "I am Kamelya of the Malachite Clan. I'll signal the others to bring the hatchlings. How long do you need?"

I cast about for a reference, then calculate. "When the sun touches that peak, I'll have my people clear."

"Very good." Kamelya stretches her wings out and I gape at the size and the colors. Blood red to bright scarlet where the thin membrane spreads between the long, delicate bones. "Let us reconvene here tomorrow evening to assess."

The dragon launches herself skywards with a whoosh and I stagger backwards, only to be steadied by Rafe. I stiffen, give him a curt nod of thanks and start down into the valley, not trusting myself to speak.

By the time we reach the others, I've regained my outward composure. The herder girl shifts anxiously. The squad hides it better, but they, too, stand alert.

"All the animals are in," Anasta reports. She grips her spear with pale, scarred fingers, the hard set of her jaw belying her mild personality. "Those that have watered are grazing by the stream."

"Good work." I nod at the others. "Move out."

We climb a narrow game trail that switches up the southern hill. This valley has been selected specifically for its steep sides and clear view of the rich grasses below. The small herd munches contentedly, their long day's march over, and I feel a twist of guilt for the carnage that is about to be unleashed. I have a soft spot for cows—my parents farmed short-horn cattle on the gentle slopes between the rivers Val and Trevi in the north of the realm. I would have likely ended up a herder myself, if I hadn't signed up to the army at fourteen.

"There's a decent-size hollow back there. Make camp, but stay alert," I order Anasta. "I want you and you," I point to Andrej and Emil, slim brothers who are my best lookouts, "stationed on that crag, and by that tree. If any of those baby dragons decide to wander up here, you alert me straight away. I'll be here in the center." The brothers salute and hustle to their appointed positions.

Anasta tells the herder girl to follow her. The other two soldiers, Pon and Stefan, are the final pair in my squad. Pon's golden skin and black straight hair marks her of Uraidlan descent, while Stefan's tall, pale countenance speaks of Trevi heritage, though with war looming everyone is too polite to say so. There are plenty of red haired Medvajans, after all.

Rafe is still standing beside me. "You may not want to watch this next bit." I give him a hard look.

He hesitates, then seems to understand, and so retreats with the others. I return my attention to the skies above the mountains, pursing my lips as the first winged shape sails into view, a squirming serpent clutched in its claws.

$\sim | \sim$

With the echoes of panicked moos still ringing in my ears, I breathe a little easier when darkness finally falls and quiet filters through the valley. A fair portion of the herd had been killed and eaten, the remaining cows huddle together under the trees, unable to escape back down the path. A huge black adult dragon blocks the way.

The hatchlings lie sated with distended bellies—tomorrow the adults would fly them back out and the next batch would be brought in—another five or so ravenous creatures to feast on Medvajan tribute.

Should I have split the herd? Or would the second lot of cows refused to have come into a valley that reeks of death? In a month's time, none of this would remain. The blood will be washed away by rain, any uncrunched bones picked clean by birds or foxes.

I've been a soldier for more than a decade, cleared out nests of bandits and hunted rogue wyrms that, until recently, preyed on our farmlands. I'll see plenty more violence before I die, especially as King Thetin keeps rattling his saber in the north.

But something about marching those cows to their death weighs on me. "Foolish," I mutter, shaking off my mawkishness as I check on the camp. I've little appetite, but force myself to eat some of the lentil stew Emil has cooked. I confirm the order of watches with Anasta and then stomp away from the circle of warm firelight, craving privacy. Out of sight of the hollow, I find a large rock to plonk myself upon, trying to get my thoughts straight.

Footsteps thought the long grass alert me to Rafe's presence. "Everything alright?" I force myself to look at him.

He approaches cautiously. "Will it bother if I sit?" He waves a casual hand at another rock—one of the many chunks of granite that stud the hillside above the tree line.

I grunt. He takes this as permission and settles down, tucking his cloak around his shoulders. I shiver despite myself. The temperature has dropped quickly.

Rafe takes his time to speak. "Possibly the bravest thing I ever saw today, ye standing and talking t'the dragon." The admiration in his voice holds no guile. "I was shitting meself, of course, but you just faced it and talked like it was… I don't know, a merchant ye were there to trade with!"

My laughter comes out as a sharp crack. "A merchant that could eat me if I shortchanged her! I could barely keep my voice steady!" It feels good to confess that, here in the dark where those I command can't hear. "I didn't feel brave," I admit, relieved he can't see my red face. "My heart almost stopped in my chest."

"Really?" Incredulous, he moves closer to peer at me in the moonlight. He smells reassuringly of cow and smoke from the cook fire.

"Really." I shrug. "When that thing took off—well, if you hadn't steadied me, I would have landed flat on my ass."

He touches my elbow, as if reminded that contact was permissible. "Didn't show. As I said, t'was a bravest thing I ever saw."

The contact lights a fire in me, a burning fueled by the terror of the dragons, and the fear of failing in my mission. I need… something, to fight, or scream or…

I turn and kiss the herder with a fierceness that rages from my bones. He doesn't hesitate, but answers in kind, meeting my need. The hand on my elbow grips tightly and while his other cups my face, lacing fingers into my short cropped hair. I bite his lip, harder than necessary, causing him to grunt in surprise, but he doesn't stop kissing. I straddle his lap, grinding and am rewarded with a stiffness I desperately need.

"Get your pants down," I demand. Climbing off him, I unlace my boots as fast as I can, then yank my breeches down and off. Rafe obliges without a word, crashing his mouth back to mine as I sink onto him with a cry of desperate relief. Astonished elation simmers in his moan.

The brief relief I feel is replaced by urgency. I clutch his arms, rising and falling as I impale myself again and again. My thighs protest after the long day's march but I ignore the ache. The satisfaction of slamming myself down is a prize worth paying for. The feeling within me builds and builds but I halt before it erupts, shifting my legs so I'm kneeling astride, still filled by him.

Rafe moans again. "I'm so close."

I give a dark chuckle and begin to rock. My hips work swiftly to a canter as I lick my two middle fingers and circle my nub in time with my rhythm. The pressure builds so swiftly this time I come with a cry, but don't cease my movements until Rafe jerks and shudders, only moments later.

Breathless, I rest my head on his chest, inhaling his sultry scent. Tiredness floods me. I close my eyes briefly, wishing I could stay like this; that I lay on a vast soft bed with pillows and sleep will overcome me as Monique kisses my forehead.

Monique? Oh shit. You just fucked the herder on the side of a hill.

Reality sinks in and I go cold. Clearing my throat, I climb off, snatching my breeches from the grass where I'd carelessly cast them. "Give me a few minutes and I'll come back down to the camp."

I can't see Rafe's expression in the dark—disappointment? Hurt? Satisfaction that he'd just gotten to swive me? He pulls up his trousers, soft leather ones likely made from the very cows he herds. They hadn't even gone past his knees. I cringe at myself.

"Er…" he begins as he laces himself up. "I heard lots of soldiers take herbs…" He trails off.

"What?" *Oh. He's worried he's put a baby in me.* "Yes, you don't need to worry about that." I sit and tug on my boots. When I say no more, he waits a moment longer, then fades back down the hill. I heave a sigh.

With both boots laced, I pull my breeches down again and relieve myself on the other side of the rock. Contraceptive herbs are readily available to men and women in the army, as well as the palace guard. Having children is as much a part of my life plans as settling down as a cow herder! I snort, relacing myself.

"So that's how humans copulate. Quite fascinating that you can do it face to face." The voice of Kamelya the dragon comes out of the darkness, and my heart almost stops.

Six

"What in all the hells are you doing here?" I hiss, outraged and mortified, and very aware that if I hadn't just relieved myself, I would have pissed my breeches.

The dragon's eyes glow in the darkness. *A predator's eyes.* But my fear curls into anger. "Well?"

"Guarding your camp, little human," the dragon speaks with no malice. The darkness I'd taken to be a huge granite boulder uncurls and starlight shines dimly on Kamelya's hide. No trace of red can be seen, the scales shine black. "Should I have announced myself during your sexual encounter? I thought it may have… killed the mood somewhat."

I sputter, incensed. "Shouldn't you be guarding from below, where your precious little hatchings lie gorged on our cattle?" My words are unguarded, but I don't care.

The dragon's head swings closer and I can make out the elongated snout beneath those fierce, burning eyes. Sharp teeth flash as Kamelya replies, "*Your* cattle? You mean the cattle that form part of the Exchange, the treaty your princess brokered?"

I don't trust myself to answer.

Kamelya sighs. "I have Dorukhan positioned below, and the rest of the wing stationed on ledges and crags around the valley. It's not just our hatchlings you have to worry about. The scent of blood will attract other predators and I take my duty to protect your group seriously, or Kyan will have my hide. Speaking of which, I wonder if he and your princess copulated face to face, since she doesn't have wings to get in the way."

"*What?*" Did I hear correctly? Had this creature just spoken about Princess Rhea and a dragon… having sex?

Kamelya sounds surprised. "You don't think so? I suppose he might just have covered her the normal way. That might be safer, even if he did use a spell to bring himself closer to her size." She continues her musing. "No other way they could have managed it, not that he said anything to me. I could smell it on him though, after the last time we brought hatchlings to feed."

I put a hand on the rock to steady myself. My heart pounds in my ears as I find my voice. "Are you suggesting *Princess Rhea*, heir to the throne of Medvaja, went and fucked… one of your kind?" Disgust and appalled fury surges in my chest.

The breeze still and quiet suddenly reigns on the hillside. Kamelya shifts and her head swings very, very close to me. Coldness imbues me, despite the heat radiating from the dragon. Those golden eyes blink over slit pupils. "You speak as though *my kind* are animals, a kind of winged lizard, perhaps. You must realize that there are some who see humans as little more than furless bears, shuffling about in the dirt. They, of course, are ignorant of how complex *your kind* are—you build and organize, seek pleasure and war. That is why we are here, after all, the result of an agreement which will benefit both races. Intelligent, capable of consent. At least, that is what I was led to believe."

Pulse thudding in my ears, I remember my position as Lead Spear of the princess' personal guard and choose my words with great care. "I spoke thoughtlessly, Kamelya of the Malachite Clan." I keep my tone measured. "If my ignorance of dragonkind has given insult, I apologize sincerely. I… was taken by surprise. Again."

The silence stretches between us. I want to close my eyes and pray that I haven't just ruined the treaty, that I'm not about to become a snack for this very large and irate dragon.

A puff of cool air stirs as Kamelya settles back on her haunches, once more a shadow punctuated only by glowing eyes. "There was no insult," she says mildly.

The breeze resumes and I find myself breathing again.

"Go back to your camp, Yatina al Stauberg. I will speak to you in the morning."

~ | ~

Sleep overtakes me reluctantly. When the sun creeps over the horizon, I drag myself from my bedroll and collect wood from the cluster of scraggly bushes down the slope. Andrej nods thanks as he coaxes the fire to life and fills a pot with water from the skins we'd topped up from the stream the day before. Breakfast is porridge made from barley, and we all eat our fill.

"What happens today, then?" Rafe asks. I hadn't spoken to him when I'd returned the night before, and it shames me, so I make the effort to be normal.

"Excellent question," I tell him, then address the rest of the group, save the two soldiers currently on watch. "The adult dragons will remove the hatchlings, then bring in another lot. I believe there are only two clutches this exchange so by nightfall we can return with any surviving cattle."

"Won't the big dragons eat them?" asks the herder girl, exchanging a look with Rafe.

I shake my head. "I've been told not." *But why not?* It seems odd to me.

"Anasta and I will take over the watch," I carry on, "then Andrej and Emil. Stay near the camp."

My squad salute, and the herder girl finds a spot to sit and whittle. She's no doubt used to sitting and waiting.

Rafe waits until I'm on watch before he approaches. I sigh. *Why is this conversation harder than all the times I've had it before?*

"It was just a one-off," I warn him, glancing at his tanned muscles and easy gait. "I don't make a habit of jumping the civilians under my care."

He crosses his arms, then shrugs. "Yer welcome t'jump again. Seems as ye needed it last night."

I curse my weakness. Yes, I'd needed it, but I have a reputation to uphold in front of my squad.

"Thank you," I manage. "Please excuse me, they're bringing the second lot of hatchlings in."

He takes the dismissal with another careless shrug. "As ye say."

Alone on the crag, I watch the black dragon—Dorukhan, I remember—lift from the valley, a shrieking wyrm clutched in each of his forepaws. As other adults swoop in and remove their charges, a shriek of moos rise from the hapless cattle. I count out every hatchling, sighing in relief when they are gone. Then I frown. Where is Kamelya? The distinct scarlet scales had not been amongst those of the adult dragons.

The answer comes in the form of wingbeats from the valley's entrance. The red dragon alights alongside me and surveys the cows who were recovering from their distress.

"That went more smoothly than I'd hoped," she declares. "This next lot will be trickier though—they wiggle faster and seem to do their best to get away. We've probably got awhile before the others return with them." She folds her wings, looking for all the world like a scaly, oversized swan. *Except with a nightmarish maw instead of a vicious beak.*

I take a deep breath. *Make an effort. The princess would want you to.* "Sounds like human toddlers."

Kamelya cranes her neck to look at me. "Toddlers? I am unfamiliar with this word."

"Older than babies. Babies crawl and can generally be contained. Toddlers have learned to walk and get into all kinds of mischief." My nieces and nephews gave my brother and his wife all sorts of trouble, and I don't miss having to help out. At least in the army there's latrine duty for those who disobeyed.

The dragon chuckles. "Toddlers indeed. These younglings have started to form wings, and it's a nightmare to wrangle them without damaging the growing bones."

"That sounds awkward," I offer, relieved at how civil our conversation is after last night.

We watch the milling cattle. There is less than a score.

"Why don't you adults eat the cows?" I ask at the same time as Kamelya says, "Did you really not know about Kyan and your princess?"

"I'm sorry, you speak." My face heats.

The dragon shakes her head. "We don't eat the cows because it's not part of the treaty. The livestock are for the younglings, to give them strength as they learn how to hunt in the mountains. Besides, most of us prefer game—it's leaner and more flavorsome. Many of the clans prefer the great fish, since we live near the sea, though the salt is not to my preference."

"Oh." *Nothing sinister after all, simply a matter of taste.* I wonder about where they live. The sea is to the south, but dragons live in the west. Unless there is another sea beyond? "Uh, no—I didn't know about the princess and… Kyan. Is he a lord, or some kind of rank in your clan?"

Kamelya cocks her head. "He is on our clan's council. Does that make him a lord in human terms?"

"Not quite…" My mind bubbles with questions. Yesterday, dragons had been terrifying, murderous beasts with the power of speech. Today… *They have councils. And knowledge of magic.* Kamelya had mentioned a spell to bring Kyan closer to Princess Rhea's size.

"Is speaking of copulation taboo to your kind?" the dragon asks. "Because you copulated with that male and today you turned him away."

"You saw that." My voice is flat. I'd been looking in the hatchlings direction, not back to where Kamelya must have been watching. "It's not taboo, I just shouldn't have done that last night."

"No? Are their rules against it?"

I start to answer, then stop. I try again. "Not exactly. My own rules, perhaps. He is a civilian in my care, so I should set an example to my soldiers so there is no question of… abuse of power." *Responsible. You need to be responsible.*

"And…" I carry on hesitantly. "I was seeing someone back in the city. Well, had started to see her. You shouldn't have more than one lover at a time. You should make it clear that you are done with someone before moving on."

And how often do you do that? A mocking voice whispers. *You get bored and start chasing the next piece of tail.*

Here were creatures that actually had tails. I can't envision how the princess… I shut the image from my mind.

"I understand the abuse of power," Kamelya surprises me by saying. "But why is it so important to not have more than one lover at a time?"

"It's… dishonorable," I say lamely. "I don't mean the princess, of course. She is very honorable, and her lovers–" I cut myself off. *Not your place to gossip about your betters!*

"You'll have to explain. Does your lover in the city disapprove of you copulating with others? That sounds quite controlling, are you sure you want to be with her?"

"Please stop saying copulating," I beg. *How in all the hells was is conversation happening?* "It's not like that, I just said I wanted to keep seeing her, so it's poor form to go and swive someone else."

Kamelya snorts, a warm, animalistic sound, which for a moment makes me think I'm standing beside a huge, scaled, winged horse… one that talks and apparently grasps ethical quandaries better than I do myself.

"Why don't you first talk to her and establish what you both want? Talk to the herder too. It's disrespectful not to."

Did I just get lectured on managing my affairs by a dragon?

I clear my throat. "Is… is that how dragons manage their…?"

"Copulating?"

I glare, then spot the curled corner of Kamelya's mouth. The dragon is teasing, *teasing* me. "You're a bit of a smart-ass, you know that?" I shoot before I can stop myself.

Kamelya thumps her tail. "Bigger brain, bigger tail. Tt's only to be expected."

I burst out laughing, not just at the comment, but at the ridiculousness of the conversation. Dozens of yards away I can see Anasta at her post, staring in consternation. I wave a hand to assure the other soldier that all was well, and my second-in-command goes back to scanning the horizon, awaiting the return of the other dragons.

"Will you be at the next Exchange?" I ask Kamelya.

Golden eyes fix on me intently. "I will. I'm apprenticed to Kyan so he wants me to learn more about humans. Your kind is… interesting."

A slow smile creeps onto my face. "I'm beginning to think the same about dragons."

Seven

These hatchlings are bigger than yesterday's, perhaps the length of two horses end to end. Another dragon flies in from the west and deposits its charge, and the feeding frenzy begins.

I find it as good as an excuse as any to leave Emil on duty and find Rafe. He's chatting to the herder girl back at the camp, standing unhurriedly when I approach and clear my throat.

"May I speak with you?"

He nods. "Aye, o'course." He pats the herder girl on the shoulder, a brotherly gesture, and follows me as we climb up from the hollow and over several boulders until I'm confident we're out of earshot of the camp.

I take a deep breath. "This is my first real command and I have a duty to acquit myself with honor. Taking advantage of someone in my care is not... how I should have behaved. And... as well as that... I'm seeing someone back in Zivalj, so this is not something I'm particularly proud of." I speak quietly, formally, forcing my voice to keep level.

When I finish, the herder nods slowly. "Yer overthinking," he says after a long pause. "Yer soldiers respect ye, and I'm no virginal lad o' lass to be swooned by the flash of a uniform. But another sweetheart, I understand. Will ye tell him?"

"Her," I correct.

Rafe's eyebrows shot up. "Does she throw plates? Had a jealous widow throw plates at me once when she thought I was sweet-talking her sister."

"I... don't know if she throws plates," I reply cautiously. "But I shall take the chance." *And clear things up with Lady Imogen. No skulking in palace corridors in case she corners you again.*

I watch Rafe lope back down to the camp, guiltily grateful he's so easygoing. *Why do I keep getting myself into these situations?* I know the answer. *The opportunity is there, and it feels good,* I think, shamefaced.

~ | ~

"Watch out!" Andrej hollers, once again stationed on the crag that overlooks the switchback.

One wyrm darts past the throng of remaining cows and shimmies up the path towards me. I lift my spear, sighting along my free arm to take aim.

With a crack like thunder, Kamelya rises on vermillion wings and the air shimmers. A gust batters the young dragon and it slips, claws scrabbling on seemingly icy ground. It skids down the slope, where Dorukhan thwacks the youngling with his tail and sends it tumbling into the stream. It snarls, then sinks its jaws into a steer already half dismembered by another wyrm. The two young dragons hiss and fight until the former abandons its prey in favor of one of the last remaining cows.

The rest of the Exchange passes without incident. Gorged and content to curl up in the sun, the 'toddler dragons' finally lie still. The adults covering the valley relax, settling down on haunches while keeping an eye on their young ones below.

"These ones ate a lot more," Anasta observes.

"Older," I reply absently, relieved I no longer have to listen to the sounds of feeding, replaying in my mind the attack of the young wyrm. *Rhea was right. The adults dealt with that far quicker and easier than we could have.* I shake out a breath, reefing my attention back to my second-in-command. "The hike back tomorrow will be quicker without the animals. We might even make Zivalj by nightfall if we leave early."

My prediction is correct. We farewell Rafe and the herder girl at Valesk shortly after midday with a respectful nod, and ride on to the capital with the practice of soldiers who are used to speed.

After seeing everyone back to their barracks safely, I report to Captain Cahill. I eye my commanding officer speculatively, wondering if he knows about the princess and her dragon lover. He already shares her bed with Prince Gereon, and while that arrangement is private from most of the court, some of the princess' household staff would no doubt have worked it out. They are loyal and well-paid, however, so I expected them to be close-lipped.

"I'd like to take the next Dragon Run," I state, stifling a yawn. *Even if for some magical reason Monique is waiting naked in my bed, I'm going to be asleep before my head hits the pillow.* "I feel confident doing it now, and formed an affinity with the council representative, Kamelya. We'd like to meet again."

Liam's astonishment gives way to a brief smirk, then vanishes into professional acknowledgement. *He does know! He thinks I'm… carrying on with Kamelya.*

Do you mean 'copulating'? The dragon's dry voice asks in my mind and I cough in embarrassment. "My squad performed well, too—I'd happily take them all again if they sign on."

"That's acceptable to me," he answers lightly. "Princess Rhea has planned a diplomatic meeting after the wedding, but the more… bonds we form with the dragons, the better, since war with Thetin seems likely."

"He hasn't backed down?"

Liam growls. "Unfortunately, the alliance with Huon hasn't deterred him. He's a wasp that keeps stinging."

I mention the pirate attacks in the river lands. Captain Cahill assures me he'll look into it, then I gladly escape to my bed. Sleep hits hard, as I expect, so my natural awakening at dawn has me groaning. I try and fail to doze.

"Get your ass up," I grumble, dragging myself from bed. My pitcher sits empty—I hadn't thought to fill it the night before—so I stump out to the courtyard pump and splash chilly water on my face.

I consider skipping morning exercises, but I need to set an example, even if my squad are excused due to our late return. *Hard work is the best cure for the restless mind,* my father always said whenever he caught me daydreaming instead of doing my chores—and the focus required to not get pummeled or whacked with practice weapons ensures I don't think about Monique until morning training is over.

Has she missed me? I wonder as I ride down the road from the palace into the city proper. Excitement builds as I draw closer. *Perhaps we could ride to the waterfall south of the city.* I smile at the thought of stealing kisses and touches—it would be too cold to swim now, the weather had certainly turned, but watching the leaves drift in to the water is universally acknowledged as a sure way to romance women. I chuckle at myself. Romance! *Into bed again at least.*

Full of these thoughts, I hitch my mount to the rail near the clockwork shop, but it is my soldier's ears that draw my attention to the raised voices inside the building. Hand on the hilt of my knife, I stride to the door and pause, listening.

"Admit it, Olaf! We gambled and we lost. We need to hawk what we can and move on." A woman's voice, like Monique's, but sharper.

"Leti, I paid three months in advance! How do you think we got a shop in such a good location? We can't just leave." The man is Monique's uncle, who sold the jewelry box to me. He sounds pleading.

"Three months?" the woman's voice rises. "That's practically all of our savings! We came here to start a new life, and you spent all of our savings straight away?" Then, in a lower voice, "We're going to starve. Once this royal wedding is over, Monique won't earn much as a dancer. We may have a roof over our heads now, but when three months run out the landlord will toss us out and it will be the middle of winter."

"Mama," Monique's voice, troubled. "I'll find work. I can draw, dance. I'll sell your and uncle's creations in the market."

"People see them as expensive curios," Monique's mother declares sharply. "Luxury items. My heart goes into every one of my pieces but nobody here values them for the art they are. We'll have to see if the Guild of Woodcrafters will let us join and repay the fee over time. It's the only way we'll get enough work to see us through, and we take a cheaper shop as soon as we can."

I push open the door, stepping hesitantly inside. Monique looks surprised. Her mother, an unhappy older version of her daughter, but of far stockier build, frowns in puzzlement.

"Ah!" Olaf beams with hope. "A return customer. You see, Leti, our clockworks will catch on!"

"Mama, this is Dame Yatina al Stauberg, Lead Spear in the princess' royal guard," Monique introduces flatly. "I met her at the palace the other week. Dame al Stauberg, my mother, Leticia Yulic. My uncle Olaf you have met already."

"An honor to meet you." I bow, unsure how to proceed. "I had hoped to speak to Monique about… her dancing up at the palace."

"Is that not the sort of thing the chamberlain organizes?" Leticia Yulic asks, perplexed. "And surely they would send a servant, not a guard." She turns worriedly to her daughter. "Monique, are you in trouble?" Back to me. "She is an honest girl, I swear it. She does not steal, nor loiter for the coin."

I blink, taken aback. "No, she's not in trouble. I, uh, just— Monique, may I speak to you?"

"It's fine, Mama," Monique assures.

"I hope your friend enjoyed the jewelry box!" Olaf calls out as we exit the shop. "Tell them to tell their friends where you got it from!"

On the street, an urchin of indeterminate sex, clad in rags and several layers of filth hovers by my horse. "Wait!" I call, when the urchin makes to scarper. "Couple of coppers to keep an eye on my mount for a bit."

"Yes, milady." The urchin bobs and holds out its grubby hand. I drop a copper in it.

"I'm not a lady, I'm a dame. The rest when I return. Don't touch the horse, he bites."

I escort Monique down the street to a vendor selling cups of lemon barley water. Several upturned barrel halves are strategically placed so customers can perch and observe the world passing by. I order drinks, and we sit.

Monique watches me. "I wasn't sure you'd be back."

My eyebrows draw together. This was not the enthusiastic greeting I'd hoped for. "Why not—didn't you get my note? I was gone less than a week."

Monique shrugs, an elegant gesture that draws my eyes to her lovely neck. I want to kiss and nuzzle and bite that neck, but Monique's next words upturn that particular apple cart of thought.

"I asked around. You don't exactly have a reputation for keeping lovers very long. I thought perhaps it was one and done."

"What?" Affronted, my fingers tighten on my clay cup.

Monique eyes me from beneath dark lashes. "You made no promises, neither did I."

"I said I wanted to see you again!"

She narrows her eyes. "Perhaps you say that to all your lovers."

Uncomfortable, I take a sip of my drink, thoughts racing. "Look, I don't normally see people for very long. It's true. I make no promises of everlasting devotion. But I'd like to keep seeing you at least a little while."

And why would that be good enough for her? You've as good as told her that you'll move on when the feelings fade. What did she call you? A clockwork soldier. No heart.

Monique stares at me with solemn eyes, then gives a small smile. "Then I shall accept the joy life gives me, not mourn its passing."

Baffled, I manage to respond, "So… you would like to keep seeing me?"

Monique's smile broadens, a radiant expression that sends flutters into my mystified chest. "Until you tire of me."

The phrase hurts. I look down. "I've no wish to hurt you, I just know what I'm like. Feelings always fade."

Monique's smile flickers. "I'll not bind you to me when that happens."

Sweet ancient gods be praised, she understands! I kiss her hand as my heart soars. "Will you be dancing again at the palace soon?" Rules be damned. I'll sneak her into my room if I have to.

"I shall." Monique's face grows grave. "However, as you may have gathered, I will be searching for work in addition to my dancing. If you know of nobles who would pay for sketches, I have quite a good hand."

I look at those elegant hands. I imagine Monique lying naked on a bed, languidly trailing said hands up her own body while I bury my face between her thighs. *Is this another way humans copulate?* Kamelya's voice interrupts.

I frown, mortified, then a completely different idea strikes. I lean forward and rest my chin on my fist. "What if you sketched dragons? I mentioned to your uncle that if he made clockworks in their shape and he said he wanted a picture. They are all the rage, but few in the court have actually seen one." My brain cautions me. Monique might claim to have a good hand, but she might be exaggerating.

"Can I see some of your work?" I ask, excited despite myself. *You don't want to promise good art only to end up with something a child would draw.* Not that *I* know anything about art, but lords and ladies at the court won't pay for rubbish.

"You can," Monique replies slowly. "But I draw from memory and life. I don't see how—"

I down my drink and stand up. "Show me your sketches. Please," I add, remembering she's not a soldier to order about.

We return to the shop. I toss another copper to the urchin and promise two more for continued vigilance. Inside, Olaf peers at us with a worried smile from his counter. "Your mother has gone out a little while. I think she is quite angry with me."

Monique kisses her uncle on the cheek. "It will be alright. We didn't come this far just to starve." She shows me through the back of the shop, into the small workroom where I wait. The smell of wood shavings and oiled metal permeates the space.

I gently touch the lave and tiny saws hanging from hooks, run my eyes over the boxes marked 'gears', 'cogs' and 'pins', as well as the tins of paint arranged neatly on the shelf. *I suppose none of these things are cheap.*

The door creaks and Monique returns, carefully holding a sheaf of papers pressed between two wooden covers. She runs a finger over the workbench, checking for dust, then lays the folio down, throwing me a perplexed look. "Are you sure this is what you wanted to see?"

"Please."

The first picture is a ship, sketched in thin charcoal, lines capturing the billow of sail as it glided from port. The second, a sailor, intent on the rope he was splicing, the ship's cat soaking up the sun on the deck next to him.

A handsome man with a roguish smile. Dolphins leaping ahead of the prow. A little girl with her hand on the neck of a dog almost taller than she was. A rider pointing from the back of their horse. Leticia and Olaf Yulic, intent in discussion on the back of a wagon. The southern gate of Zivalj, a watchmen with his head stooped to listen to an old woman leading a donkey.

"These are your travels." It's a statement. *But why?*

Monique smiles wryly. "Yes. I have a smaller book, one I carry about with me, but these are the ones I recreate from the original sketches." She hesitates, then turns the page.

It's me. Standing in the street, hand on one hip. I don't remember my smile being so flirtatious, but it seems to seduce from the page.

Monique blushes. "Some I do from memory. But I still don't see how this will help."

I touch the page gently. *Is that how she sees me?* I lift her hand and brush the knuckles with my lips. *Be careful, Yatina. You'll break her heart.* "How would you mother and uncle feel about you leaving the city for a week? I promise I'll keep you safe."

"To do what?"

I grin slowly. "To see dragons."

Eight

"King Thetin has sent raids over the border, and we've received word he plans to push south before the winter rains set in," Princess Rhea addresses us, her royal guard. "Prince Gereon and I will be marshaling our forces near Caelon and strengthening our line against the Trevi. You will all be with me, except the Lead Spear here, who will conduct the last Exchange of the season with her squad before joining us on the border."

We receive the news with stoic faces. Personally, I think Thetin a fool to attack with the weather due to change in the next month or so, but I know from overhearing conversations between Rhea and Liam that the young king is desperate to maintain his new throne from hungry lords. Uniting them to face a common enemy is an old tactic, but a good one.

"Would it be foolish to ask support from the dragons?" I query after the parade, reporting to Princess Rhea before departing. "After all, Huon is providing soldiers."

Rhea shoots me a look. "Huon shares a border with Trevault. It's in their interest to keep Thetin contained in case Medvaja is not enough. Besides, I married a Huon prince. It's a different kind of alliance."

Is it? I wonder, but keep my face neutral. "Of course, your highness."

Rhea grimaces. "Having said that, having a few dragons patrol the border would be incredibly useful for intelligence, not to mention frightening the shit out of Trevi forces. I'd rather deter a war than lose good people fighting one."

I nod. "I can raise it casually—see how it might be received?" I don't actually know if it's a good idea or not. It's all very well for Kamelya to say she has been instructed to learn about humans. Flying into someone else's battle is likely more of an education than she or any dragon wants or needs.

Rhea claps her hand on my shoulder. "I'd be grateful. I'm glad you're not terrified of them. They are more like us than you know."

I keep the straight face until after I march out, signaling the squad to mount up. Monique sits on a placid palfrey, traveling cloak wrapped around her as she watches the surrounding soldiers with keen eyes. Before the royal wedding, I had proposed to Captain Cahill and the princess that I be permitted to take an artist, to document some of the Exchange.

"Not the animals getting massacred, or anything like that," I had added hurriedly. "But me talking to Kamelya, and some of the adults in flight. It would be good for people to see evidence of their intelligence, make them less frightening."

Rhea and Liam had exchanged a look, and I suspected Liam had shared his thoughts on my interactions with Kamelya. That incensed me to some extent, but a perverse part of my mind found itself wondering how it would even work.

"Very well," Rhea had allowed. "I'll ask for a volunteer from the court artists."

"I already know someone," I'd interjected, hoping I wasn't going to be reprimanded for speaking out of turn. "She's been a dancer at the palace, but she is a very good artist as well."

Captain Cahill shrugged, lounging back in his chair. "Sounds like you've got it all worked out. How much does she want for it?"

"Oh." I hadn't thought about that part. I'd been so intent on getting Monique permission to come along, it hadn't occurred to me that a royally sanctioned artist was entitled to be paid.

"Same as the herders," Rhea had declared. "Then per piece for drawings or paintings, depending on how good they are." She had scrawled a note onto official parchment and dripped wax to affix her seal. "Have her take this to the exchequer, and pray she doesn't run away in terror the first time she gets close."

Now I wonder if Monique is already sketching the scene in her mind as we ride out. Fetchingly swathed in her blue-gray cloak, her dark hair braided sensibly, I wish she could draw a portrait of herself for me to have.

"Thank you for arranging this," Monique murmurs as we ride the road to Valesk. I had led the squad from Zivalj, but now let my bay fall back to keep pace with Monique's palfrey.

I shrug. "I'll not deny I have a vested interest in wanting to spend time with you." I hesitate. I know things will end, and that makes me sad, but I've decided to just enjoy it in the meantime.

Monique nudges her leg, causing my bay to huff and swing its head. "I like that your idea of spending time is taking me to draw pictures of terrifying creatures that could bite me in two. Very romantic."

I glare at my mount and squeeze a warning with my thighs. "Behave," I order. To Monique I answer loftily, "Some charm their paramours with poetry or flowers. I disdain such common ideas, choosing uniqueness as the flavor of my advances."

Monique's laughter draws the enquiring glances of Andrej and Emil. The brothers wink at each other and then look innocent when I snap at them to keep their eyes front.

But I can't help but let a small smile creep onto my face.

It's goats, this time, much to my relief, and only thirty in the herd. Kamelya had given me to understand that of the clutches born in summer, this was the last one that would need feeding before they hibernate in caves for the winter. Spring would see them awaken, shed scales and stretch wings that had been developing while they slept.

The 'toddler dragons', I'd learned, are past their first hibernation and will grow rapidly once they feed. They are more capable of hunting deer, wolves and bears, their ravenous appetites slowing as their awareness grows. Contact with adult dragons will become more frequent as they venture west, language developing as they are exposed to the speech of their own kind, and the desire to learn new things will draw them into different clans.

This I relay to Monique as we march up the track into the high valley, my squad spread out as they had been last time, two different herders walking amongst their charges. "I asked why they don't keep their young in caves near their parents. Apparently, they are just too feral."

"So are human children sometimes," Monique observes drily. I laugh, and she throws me that lovely smile. "But ours are far more helpless from birth, it would seem. If they had fangs and claws and could source their own food, then plenty of parents might dump them on a hillside and not let them back until they are more civilized. Apparently, I was quite the nightmare for my mother. She couldn't have done it without my uncle."

"Your… father?" I ask cautiously.

Monique presses her lips together. "Didn't even know I was born. Traveling dancer. Told her he took contraceptive herbs. She was young and hadn't sourced any for herself. Maybe he did and they didn't work, maybe he lied. I'll never know. My mother curses herself for being so naïve, but she still looks sad when she thinks I'm not looking. She says I get my nature from him. I don't think she means it as an insult."

We stop to catch our breath. "I'm sorry." I touch her on the arm.

She shrugs and smiles. "Life gives and it takes. 'We must love and mourn in equal parts, or forever fear a broken heart'," she quotes.

"Poetry?"

Monique nods. "Sonder von Aoom. My mother loves her work. She loves all Uraidlan poetry." Her eyes drift a moment, then she changes the subject. "And you? A horror of a child, or a paragon of sweetness and delight?"

Is she truly so blithe? A gnawing thought. *Or has she learned not to hold onto things?* I still don't know why they left the Breytenbach

Empire. Maybe she had to leave someone, and I don't measure up to them anyway.

Anasta passes us, giving me a salute and Monique a respectful nod. We begin our ascent again. "Youngest of seven, I don't think my parents noticed me much as long as I wasn't underfoot," I recount. "Got away with a lot. Couldn't wait to leave the farm. My oldest siblings were already having families of their own when I signed for a soldier, so losing an extra hand to help was balanced by one less mouth to feed. My next oldest brother writes me sometimes, but it's always the price of cattle, how well the hay crop did, which of my nieces or nephews have learned to walk, speak, do their numbers." I mimic Monique's shrug. "It's boring, but they seem happy. I worry about war with Trevault—they'll be in the path of fighting. I'm sure the princess won't let that happen, but I still think about it."

She nods, eyes sympathetic. "It's hard when the people you care about are in danger, but it's their livelihood at stake."

I try to work up the courage to ask her if she's speaking from personal experience when we crest the saddle. A sigh of relief goes up from all the humans, and while the goats are less desperate for water than the cattle had been, they still perk right up at the sight of the stream. The goatherds, teenage boys whose teeth are as crooked as their animals', run barefoot into the water and splash each other, laughing.

"Alright, alright," I call. "Get them watered, keep them from wandering off. Anasta, you know the drill, same as last time."

My second-in-command nods. The rest of the squad fans out, filling water skins from the upper reaches of the stream before the goats can foul it. I start to speak, then see that Andrej and Emil are already checking first that no trace of the previous month's death had been left to pollute the water. I nod with approval, then turn to Monique.

"Ready to meet your first dragon?"

Monique swallows. "Life gives and it takes." Her voice is higher than usual. "Right now it's giving an extraordinary experience, one that most people never get to have."

Pride fills my heart at her courage. "That's the spirit."

~ | ~

This time I spot Kamelya on the approach, the mammoth Dorukhan with her. I grip Monique's hand as the wind from the dragons' wings whips the air and buffets us both. Monique's errant strands of hair flick into her eyes and as usual, I'm glad mine is short.

"Seems we both had the same idea!" booms the red dragon, landing a little too close for comfort. It takes everything I have not to push Monique behind me. Dorukhan, perhaps more conscious of his bulk, alights further back, then creeps forward on huge limbs to peer at us with interest.

"The same idea?" I half-yell, the wind from their wings still settling.

Kamelya grins, showing a terrifying array of teeth. Monique draws a sharp breath. I squeeze her hand. "You brought a friend again. I told Doru about my conversations with you and he was interested in learning more about humans, too."

"Greetings," rumbles the black dragon.

"An honor," I manage, bowing. "Thank you for stopping that… young dragon when it came up the hill last time."

"You said the young ones stayed in the valley!" Monique whispers fiercely.

Dorukhan inclines his head. "Kamelya used a spell to ice under its claws. I merely discouraged it from climbing again."

So that's why it slipped. "Thank you, both of you, then." I bow again. "May I, uh, introduce, Monique Yulic—she is an artist who would like to sketch pictures of you during this Exchange."

"Pictures?" The red and black dragons turn to each other and converse briefly in a guttural tongue. Kamelya swings her head back. "Like a painting?"

Silence. I wonder if I should answer.

"Um, charcoal, on paper?" Monique offers.

More dragon-speak. "I would like to see these pictures when they are drawn," Kamelya announces. "Especially if they are of me."

"That is because you are vain." Dorukhan drawls.

"I am stunning, you bone-headed behemoth. It is no surprise they wish to draw me."

I clear my throat. Both dragons look contrite, an incredible feat for creatures as big as a cottage.

"Greetings, Monique Yulic," Kamelya says, inclining her head. "We would be delighted to have you draw us. Now— would you like to clear your people from the valley, Yatina al Stauberg, and we will bring in the younglings? There will be plenty of time to converse once they have fed. We will join you on the cliff near your camp again, and your artist can begin her sketches of me."

They take off, and Monique drags me around to face her, wide-eyed. "You never said they would... be like that!"

I hug her. "I'm sorry! I didn't know she would bring another dragon. Are you alright?"

Monique pulls free and shakes her head. "They were... just like people, except they weren't. It was like listening to neighbors bickering in the street! It was so odd!"

I grab her hand again. "Come on, I have to get everyone up out of the valley before they return. They weren't what I expected either, but... I rather like them. She's quite funny, actually, though that's the first time I've spoken to him. Or any other dragon," I add, as we hurry back down to the others. "I didn't realize they spoke something different to each other. I must ask why that is."

"All ready!" Anasta calls when we approach the knoll.

"Move out," I order, ensuring I'm the last one up the switchback. Several goats make to follow, curious about where we are going and if there are better snacking options there. The goatherds whack sticks and yell until animals decide they don't want to go that way, anyway.

"Don't watch the feeding," I warn Monique when we reach the top. "It's pretty gruesome."

She shakes her gorgeous head, pulling a sketchbook from her pack. "I want to see them fly in. I'll try not to look down."

She sets up on the grass near the top of the switchback and pulls a slender stick of charcoal from a box.

"Tell me when you see them," she requests, then begins sweeping the charcoal over paper, focused.

I watch the shapes come to life. Great curves for wings, Dorukhan peering past Kamelya's shoulder. I'm entranced by the way Monique's quick strokes bring expression into reptilian faces, and forget to keep watch.

"Dragons in the air!" Pon shouts.

"Shit!" I scan the sky, spotting Dorukhan, a smaller black dragon and a pale blue, all sporting snarling, writhing young wyrms in their claws.

Monique frantically flips to a fresh page, her charcoal skidding across the paper as she captures outlines, shapes, but no detail.

"Let's come away," I suggest. I really don't want her to see the next part.

"I'm looking up and out, not down."

"Yes, but…" *You'll hear it.* The panicked bleats begin. Goats are smarter and more agile than cattle, but even they are no match for the vicious jaws that salivate and strike. White-faced, Monique keeps sketching, determinedly flicking her gaze up as two more adults soar into view, the final younglings hissing their fury until they are released just above the valley floor, and hunger takes over their infantile minds.

Kamelya circles above, a supervisory role. I note with grim amusement that the red dragon flies past our position several times more than necessary, flaring her wings and banking for optimum view. Monique cranes her neck as Kamelya pivots on a wingtip and alights dramatically behind us.

"That little stick is charcoal? Very clever—certainly easier than paint if you are traveling light." The dragon bends her neck low, peering closely at Monique's work. "How did you get the skin so light and thin?"

I bristle at the invasion of space, ready to protect despite the ridiculous odds. Monique, clearly discomforted by the huge creature so close, makes an effort to answer politely.

"It's paper, not skin. Made from wood pulp. I believe some is made in Medvaja but the technique is from the Breytenbach Empire, where I am from." Her hands never stop—it is almost as if by sketching she is keeping a hold on her panic. Another page and the beginnings of Kamelya's head and neck take shape, with me standing next to her, hands on my hips, looking cross.

The dragon-scent is noticeable—warm, slightly metallic but not overpowering. It draws the focus though. *Hard to pay attention to anything else when such a creature looms over you!* I scowl.

"Fascinating. You work so fast! Will you go back later and fill in more detail?" Kamelya cocks her head, intrigued.

"Y-yes," Monique manages. "These are just rough sketches. I do actually paint, but this way I can get the feeling, the proportions. I'll take these back and create larger drawings, and paintings too."

"Larger? Ooh, so you could do a big one of me? I'd love to take something back to the Weyr—show my teachers. Mind you, it looks fragile. If I were to obtain a skin, could you paint it onto that?"

Monique blinks. "I could do it onto canvas." She shoots a glance at me. "The princess is paying me to draw for her so I'm not sure…"

Kamelya's vermillion crest rises. "Payment? I can pay—minerals, or bespelled crystals? Or perhaps there is something else you need that I can trade."

I interrupt, excited. "Actually there might be something you would consider!"

"Yatina al Stauberg, I was negotiating with your friend," Kamelya responds dryly. "If you have something to ask, it can be separate to this."

My jaw drops. *Did she just tell me to butt out?*

"It's alright," Monique soothes. "If there is something Yatina needs, I'd be happy to trade."

I clear my throat. "No, this is between you two." I drop my voice. "I know your family needs the money." I'm embarrassed by my thoughtlessness.

An odd stalemate hangs in the air, while Monique gives me a pained expression. The sounds of slaughter have faded from below.

"Ah," says Kamelya. "Seems like the feeding is over. They are much quicker at this age. I must check in with the others, but I shall return to negotiate my painting. And," she flashes an alarming grin, "Dorukhan has questions too. Perhaps the thing you want can be discussed then." She nudges me on the shoulder, then backs up a few steps before launching herself off the cliff. Staggering, I land on my ass in front of Monique. I take a deep breath, ready to hurl expletives.

A snort from Monique has me glaring at her instead.

"Oh, my dear, I'm sorry. You look so incensed," Monique chortles, a charcoal-smudged hand clenched to her mouth. "Your dragon is so *bossy*."

"She's not *my* dragon!" I snap, then rein in my temper. Monique doesn't deserve my ire, as much as I want to snap. "Are you going to kiss me better?" I ask sulkily, getting up.

Monique tucks the charcoal into its box and ties the book shut. She takes my calloused hand in her own soft one and presses it to her lips, her eyes still crinkled with mirth. "Later," she whispers, "I will kiss you everywhere you want."

Nine

"Your kingdom is at war?" Kamelya sounds wary and… displeased.

"Not yet," I assure her, feeling my heart sinking. "Princess Rhea and Prince Gereon are making a show of force on the border. It should deter the Trevi but… King Thetin is reportedly determined to prove his valor in battle."

"And you want a wing to conduct a flyover to frighten this king?" Dorukhan rumbles.

We sit not far from the main camp—I'd taken a branch from the cooking fire and lit our own so Monique and I can see. Dorukhan had informed us gravely that dragon eyes were extremely effective in the dark, and their hearing was greatly superior to ours.

I hesitate. "If that is something that might be agreeable to you and your council."

A guttural exchange between the dragons.

"What is it you are speaking?" Monique pipes up. "Your own language?" Her courage seems to have grown in the dark.

Kamelya grunts. "It is."

I steel myself to push the issue. I owe it to the princess. "So will you ask your council?"

"It's not our war," the female dragon answers stiffly.

I purse my lips and nod. "There doesn't have to be a war, if we can deter it. You would save countless lives."

Dorukhan lets out a long breath through his nostrils. "Our council would not condone risking draconic lives for the sake of humans. There are enough who feel these Exchanges are a mistake, and are waiting for the first opportunity to end them.”

“Really?” I stare at him in consternation. “But wasn’t it Kyan who suggested them?”

“Some feel Kyan was rash in being so conciliatory.” Kamelya bites out. “You recall me telling you that some dragons see humans as mere beasts.”

I catch Monique’s eye, who looks concerned. “You did say that…” *Well, this didn’t turn out the way you hoped, you naïve fool.* I swallow, fighting to remain gracious. “Thank you for hearing me out.” Reporting my failure to the princess is going to hurt.

“Perhaps some of my art will help convince them otherwise,” the dancer chimes in softly. “Is not art one of the hallmarks of civilization? Do dragons have poetry? Or music?”

The fire crackles and two great scaled heads look at each other. “Perhaps,” Dorukhan concedes in his deep voice. “But it would take time. Your war may begin long before that, and even then our kind would be reluctant to risk themselves for a cause that is not theirs.”

“I understand.” I hold up my hands, even as another idea occurs to me. It’s an absurd idea, but how can I face my future queen and tell her I didn’t try every option, when she herself puts her people first every time? I straighten my spine.

“The, uh, agreement that Kyan came to with Princess Rhea. Is that the kind of arrangement that dragons need to form alliances?” *Sweet ancient gods, am I really suggesting this? What if they say yes?* What would Monique say?

Kamelya bends low and sniffs me. I stiffen. “Even if the answer was yes… which it is not, Dorukhan and I do not have the authority to make such an agreement or alliance. Why?” her tone turns mischievous. “Are you curious about being with a dragon?”

Monique casts me a confused look and my face burns. I hope by all the hells that the fire light hides it. “No! I mean, a little, but,” I look guiltily at Monique, “not me. I just needed to know if that would help.”

“My dear, what are you talking about?” Monique asks suspiciously. “What does Kamelya mean ‘being with a dragon’?”

Dorukhan chortles. "Kam told me humans copulated as much for fun as our kind does. Neither of us knows the shrinking spell, though, so it might be limited."

"Copulated?" Monique's dark eyebrows rise to her hairline.

I regret ever being born. "Forget I said anything. We should sleep."

Dorukhan nudges his counterpart. "We should... *sleep*, too, Kam. Isn't that what you said humans called it? Funny, because you would think you have to stay awake for it."

The red dragon laughs, a raucous sound that makes me wish she was human size so I could punch her. "*Sleep* well, little humans."

The fire gusts as both dragons open their wings and take off into the darkness. I wonder if they'd sneak back later in the hope of witnessing human copulation.

Voyeurs, I snarl in disgust, avoiding the gaze of the woman next to me.

"Yatina?"

"Mm?"

"What was that about?"

Oh, nothing. Those two dragons are perverts, that's all.

"Yatina."

Argh! I sigh. "I need to swear you to silence. This is not my secret to tell. I never wanted to know it, but if the Princess can make sacrifices for her country, then so can I."

She grazes my arm. "You have my silence. But... were they saying... are you implying that the princess and a dragon..."

"Kyan," I answer miserably. *You couldn't keep your big mouth shut, could you? What kind of loyalty is that?* "I shouldn't have said anything. What the princess does is her business, even if it's not normal."

"Yatina." Monique touches my elbow and forces me to look up. Reflected firelight shines in her lovely dark eyes. My mouth goes dry. Despite several days of rough travel, she trumps the dirt and frizzled braids. "I'm not horrified, if that's what you're worried about."

I scrunch up my nose. "You're not? But… I mean, firstly, the princess is married to Prince Gereon." *Don't mention Captain Cahill.* "And… Kyan is a *dragon*."

A smile tugs. "On the eastern coast of the empire, fisherfolk take lovers amongst the merfolk who live there. I'll admit the size difference had me perplexed, but Kamelya and Dorukhan mentioned a shrinking spell?"

I nod.

Monique shrugs. "Then I'm intrigued." She smiles wickedly, and it does strange things to my chest. "Does that make me a bad woman, thinking about such scandalous things?"

Heat floods me. I lean in close. "It does," I breathe. "But I don't entirely mind it." Quite the opposite, it thrills me that she is so adventurous.

She traces a finger down my arm. "And were you asking before about an arrangement with the dragons?"

I cough. "I was just asking. I didn't necessarily mean for me."

"No?"

Does she sound… disappointed? "I mean, if it was required, I'd do my duty," I answer carefully.

She laughs. "Always so serious!" She pushes me gently. "Aren't you curious?"

I stare, then sweep an arm around Monique and tip her back. Lying atop, I stare intently into those eyes. "You really are a bad woman," I say incredulously. "You have the most wicked thoughts!" Excitement courses through me.

Monique kisses then nips my lips. "Pleasure is pleasure. Perhaps it's not the art or the poetry that align us, but the seeking of enjoyment." She runs a hand down to my buttocks and squeezes. I growl. Monique laughs. "You sound like a dragon," she teased.

"Do not." I growl again and bite gently at her neck. Monique gives a half-sigh, half moan that courses lightning straight to my core. I work one leg between Monique's and grind against her, kissing and biting gently. Then I remember what she said about different ways, and inspiration strikes.

I rise to kneeling, then pull Monique up and guide her to her knees, facing the embers. Behind her, I grip her waist, working my fingers under the jacket and the shirt. I continue to drag my teeth along her neck.

"You're very skilled at exacting pleasure from me," I murmur. "I imagine you'd take pleasure from a dragon just as well." I bite softly, letting my fingers tease the soft skin of Monique's waist. "Let it cover you, perhaps? On your knees, up against a rock?" Monique's breath comes faster. "I thought you were such a sweet girl," I go on.

"You… like… my… sweetness," she moans, trying to tease.

"I do. I want it on my tongue, my lips, my fingers. I love your scent." Tempted as I am to reach further around and down, I resist and continue to trail my fingers from the top of her hips to the smaller of her back. "You are a sweet girl, but also a very wicked one, and I like that too."

Monique starts rocking, and I marvel at how aroused she is.

"You make such lovely sounds when I touch you and taste you," I whisper, realizing I elicit a stronger whimper every time my thumbs trace near her spine. "I like hearing you moan, feeling you shake apart when I make you… come." I bite harder, right on the side of her neck just as I grip hard with my hands and am rewarded with a deep groan of pleasure. My gorgeous lover shudders and falls backwards against me. I cradle her, enraptured.

"You're wonderful, so incredible the way you do that," I tell her, kissing her forehead and hair. "It has to be magic. No normal person can come like you do."

Monique gives half a chuckle. "I'm glad… you think so," she manages, smiling sleepily up at me. My heart swells.

"I'd better get you to bed." I help her to her feet, smiling as I straighten her clothes. Then I stop as the memory I've been avoiding crawls into the front of my mind.

You still *haven't told her about Rafe*. I squirm as my conscience does some fancy footwork justifying keeping my mouth shut versus being honest.

But if you don't tell her about Rafe, Kamelya might. A nagging voice reminds me. *And you shouldn't avoid doing the right thing just because you're afraid of getting caught out and looking bad.*

"What's wrong?" yawns Monique, cuddling into my side.

"Nothing!" I'm utterly unconvincing, and despite her sleepiness, she frowns.

"Are you worried about your reputation with the others? I'm pretty sure they've worked out there is something going on between us."

"It's not that." Guilt gnaws at me.

"Are you sure? I know what your reputation means to you."

"You do?"

Monique chuckles softly. "You were so proper that first time at the shop. So worried about behaving correctly. I know you take your position very seriously—it's clear in the way you speak about the Princess, or your captain, or the soldiers under you. You're very honorable."

Guilt floods me. "I'm not, always. I… I made a mistake last time I did the dragon run."

"Oh?" Monique teases. "Did you insult a dragon?"

Well… "Uhhh, yes, but that wasn't the big mistake." My guts clench and I blow out my cheeks. *Stop being a coward.* "I, uh, I slept with one of the herders. It was a very quick thing, I was very tense from meeting with Kamelya, and the feeding was awful, the poor cows were terrified, and he thought I was brave and we fucked and then I regretted it because I was there to look after civilians not take advantage of them and I knew I wanted to see you when I got back, and then the fucking dragon had been sitting there in the dark the whole time and called me out on it and I was mortified and I…" I pause and take a breath.

"I meant to come and tell you when I got back but forgot because it really wasn't important. I mean, the sex wasn't, telling you was." It all pours out in a horrible rush and the bliss and serenity I'd been feeling saps away, leaving this shameful, hollow pit in my stomach.

Monique is silent, cocking her head. "You had sex with one of the herders."

"Yes." *Ah, tits. This is where she storms off?* Would she call me names? Slut? Harlot? Or would she simply press those soft, full lips together in a tight line and return to camp, radiating disappointment and disgust?

"Took advantage?"

I sigh. "He wasn't unwilling. He offered again afterwards, but I explained I… I had someone in the city I was seeing."

Monique's eyebrows rise. "We hadn't discussed it at that point."

"I know, but I wanted to keep seeing you, which is unusual for me, which I guess is why I forgot in the moment." *Just like you forgot about Lady Imogen the moment you saw Monique that night…* a nasty voice whispers. I quash it. I would deal with that soon. There is only so much shame I can hang out like wet laundry this night.

"Tell me again… slowly. Did he have a name?"

"Rafe." I pause. "He wanted to see dragons, and needed the money to send home to his family in the river lands. They'd suffered from pirate raids and are trying to rebuild."

"And you were afraid from meeting the dragons."

I close my eyes. "I was. I'd never been so close. It wasn't until afterwards when I really started talking to Kamelya. I…" I wince "I made the mistake of insulting her—I didn't realize how like people they are. They *are* people, just huge, winged, smartarse people who rule by council and get frustrated with their young and study and get bored and *do magic*." I throw up my hands.

Monique's lips twitch. "They really are."

I turn my gaze mournfully to hers, the fading firelight throwing shadows across her face. "I know it was wrong."

She sighs. "You were afraid. This herder thought you were brave, you… had a passionate encounter, and then you regretted it. Was it good?"

I flush. *A passionate encounter. Better than copulate, I suppose.* "Yes. It was quick, but… yes, it was good."

"And you felt bad because you have a reputation to uphold?"

"I did the wrong thing!"

Monique sighs. "Did anyone get hurt?

"Aside from the cows, no."

"Do you plan on doing it again?"

"No! I just…"

"You just?"

A big sigh. "I don't always think before I do things."

"Seems to me like you think an awful lot."

I glare. "Afterwards, yes. But before? I can't seem to help myself, like when I met you by the fountain. It was reckless. I'm supposed to be responsible as Lead Spear. But I keep doing stupid things."

"Am I a stupid thing?"

"No!" Horrified, I blurt, "I didn't mean that. See? I say stupid things too, hurtful things. If we keep seeing each other, I'll just end up hurting you because… these feelings won't last. They never do—usually once I've slept with someone I'm not interested anymore. And if I try… well, I don't stay faithful."

Way to kill the mood, Yatina. Even a voyeuristic dragon wouldn't have done so well.

"Yatina, do you want to end this now?"

"No." It's almost a whisper.

Monique strokes my cheek. "Then just promise you will tell me when you do want to end it. I won't shriek, or weep. Just tell me."

I'm filled with such overwhelming sadness that I bite my lip hard. *I don't deserve her kindness.*

"I promise." I kiss her on the lips, knowing myself false but unable to say anything else. I cannot give her up just yet. The contradiction hurts my head—that I want her so badly but know my fickle heart will turn at some point. It's part of my nature.

She caresses my cheek. "I won't let you hurt me."

I look at her oddly. The fire has almost died and I can't make out her expression, but no one has ever said that to me before. It takes some of the pressure off.

"Come, now," she links her arm through mine. "Let's not mourn something that yet lives."

~ | ~

"You shall return on the next Exchange?" Kamelya asks Monique, her tail swishing excitedly as we make our farewells two mornings later. I raise my eyebrows. *Someone is keen for their artwork.*

"I shall." My dark-haired beauty beams back, and I feel a pang in my chest at how lovely she is, standing in the sunlight, cheerfully facing a giant creature who I would have screamed at and attacked not so long ago. *How things change.*

I clear my throat. "I had an idea about how we might… send out a call to you if it's not a prearranged time." I'm careful not to use the word 'summon'.

Dorukhan peers at me with interest. "How?"

I lift the battle horn that hangs from my belt, having retrieved it from my pack. "You said your hearing was far better than humans. How far away could you hear something like this if I blew it?"

Both dragons sniff the horn and consider. "Many leagues," rumbles the black dragon. Kamelya nods.

"Try it next time you come. I shall ponder on a better way of sending messages. Perhaps there is a spell Kyan knows."

With that, she bows once more, blows a quick blast of warm air over Monique and takes off, Dorukhan on her tail.

I gaze at Monique, eyebrows raised. "What was that about?"

She blushes. "I have no idea."

Ten

The next two weeks is a blur of final preparations for Rhea and Gereon's wedding, late night ardent embraces with Monique in whatever corner or room we can find, early morning training and meetings, meetings, meetings in between. *Seriously, some of these meetings could have been a message.* Another dragon run is scheduled to take place right after the wedding, and reports continue to come in from the northern border that King Thetin is moving troops into the area.

I'm burning the candle at both ends, but so is everyone else right now. All the visiting dignitaries have arrived, diplomats from Uraidla and Huon, as well as the Empire. No one from Trevault, and I don't have to be a political mastermind to know that's a snub.

It's a relief when the ceremony finally takes place and Rhea and Gereon emerge from the shrine, the blessing of King Denusake upon them. The court celebrates and so does the rest of Zivalj, the roaring approval of the city folk echoing when the bells are rung to signal the nuptials have concluded. Banquets are laid out in the street, food and wine sent down from the palace. Monique, along with every other dancer, acrobat and performer from near and far, have been pressed into service to entertain in a spectacular parade that winds down into the city, looping through the major streets then back up to the palace with the prince and princess riding white horses bedecked with blue and green ribbons.

I'm on parade duty too, riding in front to ensure the way is kept clear. I'm glad I had my dress uniform cleaned weeks ago—it's the exact sort of thing I usually remember at the last minute. Monique is further back in the train, but I hope she catches a glimpse of me looking so fine. Even my boots are shined to within an inch of their life.

Thinking of Monique has me clench the saddle with my thighs and my mount skips before I force my seat to relax.

I'm aching for her. A snatched kiss here and there is not enough. Tonight I plan to sneak her into my room in the barracks, consequences be dammed. Well, I say that, but of any night to be reckless, tonight is my safest wager, with the whole palace reveling.

It's the interminable work of hours to finish the parade and stand honor guard as Rhea and Gereon reenter the main gate. They dismount and stride gracefully into the palace, where the celebratory banquet awaits. The kingsguard takes over and I follow the procession into the great hall.

Sweet ancient gods, I'm so happy for them, but could this day drag on any longer? Although not on duty, it would appear remiss if I wasn't present to eat and drink the royal couple's health. So many toasts, so many speeches, and gifts from emissaries, and gifts from nobility, and well wishes from the elected wardens of towns across the kingdom. I'm fighting the urge to drink, anything to make the time go faster.

Finally, I think I can sneak out unnoticed.

"Dame Yatina!"

Ah, shit. "Lady Imogen." Now I'm glad I haven't been drinking, because I'll need my wits to avoid giving offence. "How lovely you look this evening." She does—her blonde ringlets cascade into the cleavage of her low cut dress, and I'm fighting to keep my expression neutral. *Think of Monique!*

Lady Imogen flutters a breathy laugh. "You are too kind. You, yourself, look very dashing. I heard you rode at the front of the parade today! My friends and I would love to hear you tell of it."

Is she… are they just bored *and I'm their entertainment?* My eyes narrow for a moment, then I give her a bland smile. "Forgive me, perhaps another time. I am quite fatigued by the day."

She pouts. "Surely you cannot be leaving! This is the greatest celebration our court has had for years! You must stay and enjoy!"

Her simpering irritates me. "Please excuse me," I bow and hurry out, praying she finds someone else to distract her. I cannot afford the ill-feeling of a court lady if she decides to speak against me to the princess.

But I'll take the chance right now. Because my lover is waiting.

~ | ~

A small cry escapes Monique as I grasp her thighs and hoist her up, carrying her to my bed. We've slipped into my room in the barracks, and I bless the privacy afforded to me by my rank as Lead Spear, because I strip off as fast as I can, then almost rip her from her clothes.

"Slow down!" she laughs, shimming free. "You'll tear my dress!"

"I don't care. I'll buy you a new one," I growl. "I've been going crazy for you all day. I want you sitting on my face."

Her eyes sparkle wickedly. "I saw you up there today, sitting on your fine horse. Now look at you, ordering me about."

"Please!" With that I fall back and pull Monique onto me. She laughs as I hustle her to crawl up. Arranging her legs on either side of my face, I inhale her warm scent, then kiss and lick my way into her sweet center. She jerks and gasps, but I grip her gorgeous, muscled thighs tightly.

I kiss again, sweeping through her folds and onto her nub. "Yatina!" Her accent strengthens as she chokes out my name.

"Sssh," I soothe and kiss slowly. "No one can hear you!" I'm taking a dreadful risk having her here.

She tries to comply, but I undermine her control with each roll of my tongue. "Please," she begs.

I grin, the taste of her on my lips. "Please what?" Licking again, she starts.

"Please," she almost sobs. "It's so much!"

I slow my kissing again, up and down, avoiding the most sensitive part. Little mewling cries escape her, but she doesn't pull away as I place kiss after passionate kiss on her lips. I tease a lick over her nub and she stifles a shriek, then I plunge my tongue into her and hold on tight as she bucks hard, head thrown back. Every sense of mine delights in her—scent, taste, feel, look, sound. Above me, she is a goddess.

A ragged chuckle escapes Monique, and she gives me a look I can only describe as intoxicated, though there is not a whiff of liquor or wine on her. She slides down and I cradle her as aftershocks shudder their way through. I breathe her in, feeling her heartbeat against my chest.

"It was a beautiful wedding," she murmurs later, tracing circles around my nipples, then bending to suck them gently.

"Oh! Mmm, yes, beautiful." I reach for her, only to have my hand pushed away.

"Oh no," she admonishes. "You're going to lie there and let me explore you. I want to take my time."

I work hard to stay still. It takes all my discipline to not stir restlessly as Monique teases with her lips and brushed fingertips around and over my nipples. I refuse to beg, but the pooling of heat causes my hips to cant, aching for the attention to divert there.

Monique's breathing starts to come harder, her tongue flashing out and stroking as she rolls her palm over the other nipple. She switches back to the first nipple and moans, eyes closed. I fight the urge to reach down and touch myself, touch her, touch something, dammit!

Monique moans again, a deeper sound, the vibration tingling through my breast. She sighs, closing her eyes and becoming still. She rests her dark head, glimmering with beads of sweat, on my chest, smiling like she's the cat with the cream.

"Did you just come *again*? With your *mouth?*"

Monique nods, smug, then drags her fingers down my firm stomach, teasing the shaved-short hairline.

"Unbelievable." My breath comes in short snatches as Monique traces lower and lower.

"See? Even now I bet I could bring you to the edge just from touching? Have you ever taken the time to explore?"

"Usually... I just... want to... *fuck*—" I groan as she dips into my wetness, circling back around my nub.

The beautiful creature chuckles, swirling back and forth, feeling my nerves get harder with each brush past. I fight the urge to grab Monique's hand and force her fingers into my quim so I can ride myself to climax. *Patience,* my mind commands. *Are you brought to pieces so easily?* Sweet ancient gods, if we make love like this all the time, I don't think I could ever get bored.

Finally I come, drawn out and trembling. Monique hums into my neck as we lay, entangled, our breathing slowly falling into rhythm.

~ | ~

I wake. *Why am I so warm?* Oh, there's a body in the bed next to me. It's a cheap, narrow cot, so we're squished together. I don't mind it, because it's Monique's steady breathing that I can hear, the scent of her skin that fills my nostrils. I like it.

My eyes fly wide. My tensing disturbs her.

"Yatina?" she mumbles.

I kiss her forehead. "It's okay." We must have fallen asleep. I knew everything would catch up with me. *Dammit.*

She yawns. "I'm sorry. Is it dawn?"

My eyes flick to the gray light inching through the shutters. "Yes. I'm sorry. We need to go soon."

Someone hammers on the door. "Dame Yatina, are you in there? We're already saddling up." It's Anasta.

Ah, crap. "I'll be there shortly!"

A pause. "Is Mistress Yulic with you?"

My eyes slide sideways. She raises a coy eyebrow. "She is," I answer levelly. "We were just discussing logistics."

A pregnant pause. "Of course. We'll see you in the courtyard shortly."

Fully dressed and mounted up, I am careful not to look at Monique as we ride out the gate. I maintain the illusion as we ride to Valesk, fighting the urge to gaze over, or drift back in the column to loiter near her. It drives me to distraction, but I manage to pretend to be calm and in control and set a good example to my squad even though all I want to do is sweep Monique back to bed and not leave it for a week.

"Good t'see yer again, Dame al Stauberg." At Valesk, my discomfort is compounded by the fact that Rafe is once again herding cattle as part of the Exchange.

"Ah." I dare a glance at Monique, but she is further back in the group, looking tired on her palfrey. "And you, Herder Rafe. Ready to move out in the morning?"

In the inn, I manage to sneak several moments of conversation with Monique. "Gorgeous, I'm sorry I've barely spoken to you all day." The urge to hold her is overwhelming.

She gives me a tired smile. "I was worried, at first, then I reminded myself you're trying to maintain your reputation with your soldiers."

Relief floods me. "Thank you for understanding. It's awful, having to pretend."

"Would it be so bad if they knew? Some of them surely suspect."

I clear my throat. Someone thumps down the stairs and passes us in the hall. "Be sure to make the sketches the princess wants tomorrow," I say loudly.

Monique raises an eyebrow ironically and I feel stupid.

"Rafe is also on this dragon run," I tell her in a lower voice. "Nothing is going on there, but out of respect, I wanted to let you know. Especially if Kamelya brings it up."

"Why would she bring it up?"

A shout from the taproom. I frown. It doesn't sound like one of my squad but I'd better go investigate just in case. "Because she's a busybody. Look, I'll be able to talk more once we're up there, under the guise of guarding you." I peck her cheek.

"Yatina."

I'm half way through the door when she speaks. I turn.

She gestures with her hands. "If you do want something to happen with Rafe, just tell me," she says softly. "I'm not here to stop you."

I go to reply, then hear another shout—this time definitely one of my squad. I break up the argument in the taproom between Stefan and a local who has taken a dislike to him, and by the time I've checked on the horses and gear, Monique has gone to sleep. I creep into the room I'm sharing with her, Pon and Anasta and lay out my bedroll closest to the door.

The next day we make the familiar trek into the mountains. The cows are settled into the valley and I blow the horn to alert the dragons to our presence.

"Not bad!" Kamelya calls as she circles in to land. "Kyan gave me something to magically amplify it." She reaches into a pouch that hangs from her left fore-paw, and proffers a leather band etched with symbols. "Wrap this around it, and when you blow it I will hear if I am wearing the matching pair." Another leather band adorns her wrist.

Before I can answer, she lowers her head to Monique, who stands next to me. "How nice to see you again, Monique Yulic. Have you any paintings for me?"

Monique smiles. "Not yet, I'm afraid, but I want to show you the drawings I made from last time, and you can select your favorite for me to paint."

"Can it wait until the feeding has taken place?" I interrupt pointedly. What is it with these two and usurping the conversation?

Kamelya casts me an amused look. "By all means."

~|~

When Rafe comes to speak to me about the status of the herd, Monique gives me an encouraging smile from her nearby perch where she sketches. I frown. Doesn't she know I'm just aching to get her alone again?

"A little more than half remain." He bows respectfully, but gives me a wink as he looks up. "May I invite you to inspect them?"

I really don't want to, but can't expect anyone else in the squad to do such an unpleasant task. Monique is absorbed in her work again, so Rafe and I stroll the top of the cliff as I check his count of live cows against gorged, sleeping baby dragons. My stomach churns.

"And how go things for ye, Lead Spear?" Rafe enquires. "We heard o' the princess' grand wedding. The country rejoices for her."

"Indeed." At least the wind carries the scent away from us tonight. Seeing splashes of blood and scraps of mangled cow hide are enough to add to my already unhappy mood. Monique seems to be taking my guise of being disinterested too seriously—every time I try to snatch a word with her, she's distant, or busy speaking to the other soldiers. The sun will set soon and I haven't been able to organize a rendezvous.

What did she mean, if I wanted something to happen with Rafe? All three of us together? Normally I wouldn't object to the suggestion, but something is off and I can't put my finger on it.

Rafe is clearly more intuitive than me, because he doesn't try for more conversation and we return to the camp without another word.

"Where's… Mistress Yulic?" I ask, a little more strident than necessary.

Anasta points up the hill. "Talking with the red dragon." Even my squad are more comfortable with the idea of dragons as people now. The Exchange has gone from a deadly gauntlet to a routine patrol.

I hasten up the hill, past the scrubby bushes and large boulders that protect the camp's hollow from the biting wind that whistles now in the pink-orange late-afternoon light. Finally, I'll get to speak with her alone! I mean, Kamelya doesn't really count.

I skirt a final boulder and halt. My jaw drops. My lover sits with her back to Kamelya's chest, eyes closed in bliss, while the dragon, lying on her side, nuzzles Monique's neck and hums.

I swallow to stop my jaw from dropping. I know that look. I've brought it about myself multiple times, in ways I never would have expected.

Kamelya and Monique...

My brain tries not to combust as I back behind the boulder and stay, peeking out.

There's nothing... overtly sexual in their positions, save the neck nuzzling. But Monique's radiant expression makes my stomach flip excitedly. I want to go to her, but that would rate high on the list of 'stupid things' so I slip away silently, glad the chill wind blew towards me and Kamelya couldn't scent me as easily.

I pull my cloak tightly around me and return to camp, not speaking as I sit near the fire and think. I accept a bowl of soup from Emil and let the warmth of the flames soak into me as realization soaks into my mind.

This is why she was encouraging me with Rafe. She... she is like Princess Rhea, desirous of more than one lover at a time. It's why she was so unfazed by my declarations of struggle when it comes to fidelity. Why she didn't shriek and cry when I told her about Rafe.

Why didn't she say something sooner? Then I think of how ashamed I was when I told her about Rafe. How judgmental I must have sounded when I spoke of the princess. She must have known I needed to be eased into the idea.

But now the idea strikes me with force and I'm reeling at the implications. Respect, affection, without being trapped.

Monique returns to the camp shortly after and thanks Emil for the soup. I give her a smile and a nod, showing her I understand. She returns the smile uncertainly.

"I've told Kamelya I'll have her painting done in a month." She blows on her spoonful, but the rapidly dropping temperature renders such precautions unnecessary. She shivers, and I wonder why she isn't wearing a thicker cloak.

"That's excellent," I say. "May I see some of your sketches from today?"

She glances away. "I'm very tired. Tomorrow?"

I chuckle internally, knowing why she's tired. It drives me wild, but I bank my own lust. I won't be scratching that itch with Rafe, even with her encouragement. It's Monique that I want, when she is ready.

"Of course," I wink. "You need your rest."

~ | ~

Bathed in the pink sunrise, Monique sits cross-legged on a rock, sketching the valley below. She is blissfully unaware I'm gazing at her, taking in her raven hair, smiling softly as I watch the way she concentrates, hand gliding across the paper.

The feeling I have is more than lust. I know this now. Affection and gratitude compete as I think about how lucky I am to have met her, how kind and patient she has been with my shortcomings. She has opened my eyes to the possibility of love.

My ruminations screeched to a halt as danger creeps into the vision of loveliness in the form of a young, dark brown dragon.

The distance between Monique and me stretches out as the creature emerges from the bushes on the far side, intent on its prey. A thousand thoughts scrambled through my head. *How did it get up here? Where's Kamelya? I don't have my bloody spear!*

"Look out!" I holler.

Yanking the rope dart from my belt, I spin the cord, time seeming to slow as Monique's face flashes alarm and the young dragon snarls, a noise that reverberates the lungs and chills the spine.

Monique leaps to her feet, sketches and charcoal scattering. She stumbles just as the dragon pounces and I release my dart at the perfect point in its arc.

The sharpened steel punctures the dragon's eye and it shrieks, lashing in pain. Monique crawls towards me, white faced.

I yank back the dart and spin again, ready to make the kill.

A clap of thunder knocks me off my feet. Dark wings blot out the sun and for a moment I thought I'd been knocked out. But I'm still conscious. The young dragon wails, high-pitched and furious, but the sound is farther away. I cast about frantically, piecing together the chaos.

Dorukhan has picked up the young dragon and is flying away. Monique, still on her hands and knees, reaches me. I drop and grab her tightly, patting her down.

"Did it get you? Where are you hurt?"

Monique, face paler than a page in her sketchbook, shakes her head. "I'm fine, I rolled my ankle. It didn't get me." She sinks to the ground and I rise, desperate to comfort but afraid to let down my guard.

Vermillion wings flap and Kamelya lands. "What happened?" the red dragon demands.

I tensed. "One of the younglings must have woken early and climbed the cliffs. It attacked Monique. I defended her."

Kamelya's great head sways back and forth, sniffing.

"I see. Monique Yulic, are you injured?"

"I'm fine. Will it be alright?" Monique asks. I glare. I don't particularly care if the beast is alright. I'm incensed the adult dragons let it get past their guard.

"I will go and check. You are hurt." Kamelya peers down at Monique, who winces as she tried to stand.

"Just my ankle. I'll be fine. It didn't actually touch me."

"Hmm." Air rushes across us as the red dragon takes off, leaving Monique running her hands through her disheveled hair and me blinking the dust from my eyes.

"This is not good, is it?" Monique looks anxiously up at me.

"It'll be fine!" I try to soften my voice when she looks alarmed. "Don't worry, I won't let them hurt you."

"I don't think they would…" her voice quavers uncertainly. "Yatina, I don't think I can walk. I've hurt this ankle before. It usually takes days before I can use it."

I feel a pit in her stomach. "We'll make a litter. It's fine."

"A litter won't get me down this cliff. It's too narrow."

"Then I'll carry you!"

Monique swallows. I feel guilty for yelling.

I kneel next to her and kiss her forehead. "I'm going to fix this." I'm embarrassed to find tears leaking from my eyes. I feel sick. Monique, patient, generous, beautiful Monique, had very nearly been killed.

"I will get you safely back home," I vow. "I swear it."

Eleven

"I don't know when we will see you again," I admit stiffly to Kamelya. Dorukhan and the other dragons have already disappeared into the mountains with the hatchlings. The one that had attacked Monique will live, I've been told. I hide my lack of concern behind the guilt that I may have jeopardized the treaty.

"There are no more Exchanges until spring, but I have spoken to Monique Yulic about delivering my art in a month's time," the red dragon responds despondently. "Kyan and Dorukhan and I will come to the place you call Valesk at the new moon. If you are there, I will see you." She doesn't meet my eye. Perhaps guilt over the attack eats at her, too.

I turn to Monique and shrug helplessly. "I will be ordered to the front upon our return. Trevault is poised to attack our border and I must defend it."

Monique bows to the dragon. "I will see you at Valesk, Kamelya." Despite her pain, she sounds genuine. I wonder at her capacity for forgiveness, feeling ashamed of my own burning to eviscerate the thing that almost killed her.

I brood as we hike down out of the valley. Monique remains uncomplaining as she's jerked and jolted on the makeshift litter. Our progress is painfully slow. Some way out from Valesk, clouds roll over and a light drizzle begins.

"Yatina," Monique begs. "Please don't make them trudge through the rain for me. Go ahead and come back with a horse or donkey or something."

Appalled, I snap, "Don't be ridiculous," then I catch the sideways look Emil gives his brother. My lip curls, and force out the order, "Go ahead to Valesk and return in the morning with our horses. I'll wait with Mistress Yulic."

We sit under the sparse autumnal cover of an elm tree, cloaks pulled tight, unspeaking. I glance at Monique's clenched jaw and curse myself silently for letting this debacle unfold.

If you'd been awake earlier. If you'd told her to stay in camp. If you hadn't stopped to stare and daydream like a moon-eyed fool!

I'm angry at Kamelya too, for not being there sooner, for dismissing me so coldly when I'd had explained the situation. *You were supposed to run everything smoothly, and you messed up!*

I dread reporting this to Captain Cahill and the princess. The dragons would never consider lending their aid to the Medvaja—not after I'd almost killed one of their younglings. *You got distracted, again, and this happened.*

I steal another glance at Monique, who still sits silent. "Are you in much pain?" My voice is rough.

A tight-lipped smile. "It's fine. I've done this before. It usually heals in a few weeks."

"A few weeks?" I'm horrified. "But you won't be able to dance!"

Monique closes her eyes. "I know."

Shit. I rub my eyes. Yes, Monique would have her paintings to do, but that would take time. Dancing, whether at the palace or elsewhere, paid immediately.

"I'll sort something out," I promise.

"You don't have to 'sort something out'." The sharp tone shocks me. "You're not responsible for me. And besides, aren't you going to the border as soon as we're back? You're not going to be around."

Hurt, I clench my jaw and don't answer. I watch Monique shivering and think with annoyance. *She really should have brought a thicker cloak.*

"Would you like my cloak?" I offer gruffly.

"No, thank you." Her accent clips her words.

It's a very long night.

~|~

Anasta and Stefan arrive mid-morning and despite the swelling on her ankle, Monique manages to sit in the saddle. We don't talk. I'm confused and every time a thought bubbles to my lips, I push it down. I've messed up. I don't want to make it worse.

More gray clouds drift in from the south, but the rain holds off until we reach the palace. I barely see the salutes the guards give her, going over in my mind how I am going to present my report to Captain Cahill.

Who isn't there. I slap myself mentally—the captain, along with the Princess' entire personal guard, has already ridden north to Caelon to reinforce the army outpost there.

"Dismissed," I bark to Anasta and the others. "Be prepared to leave in the morning." I will have to find the captain of the king's guard, a dour middle-aged man who barely utters a word when he doesn't have to. *Probably for the best.* I look around and find Monique has already dismounted without waiting for my help, and is hobbling to a bench near the small gatehouse that guards the stables' main courtyard.

"If you are able to wait, I'll make my report and escort you back to the city," I tell her, frowning at her obvious pain.

"Dame al Stauberg!" a shriek of delight assaults my ears. Dread presses upon me as Lady Imogen flutters out of the palace and beams. "My dear brave dame," Imogen simpers. "How you have been missed at court! You must tell of your adventures." She advances and kisses both of my cheeks, oblivious to my stiffness.

"Lady Imogen." A shallow bow. "Forgive me, I must make my report to Captain Greyvensteyn."

"Of course, of course!" Imogen drapes her beringed hand on my forearm. "But you must sit with me at dinner again now you're back—with everyone gone away to war it's terribly dull at the palace and you… well, you are exciting." She winks.

I don't dare look at Monique. *Why must Imogen appear now, of all times!* "Please excuse me, my lady." I disentangle myself, red-faced, and march straight into the palace.

Greyvensteyn is in his office, a stern, plain room that reflects the occupant's personality well. He accepts my report without comment and advises that my orders are indeed to ride north the next day. I hasten back to the stables.

Monique is nowhere to be seen.

"You! What's your name? Joshu," I address a hostler. "Did you see where the lady who was sitting here went? Black hair, she had an injured foot."

Joshu stares at me, leaning on his hayfork.

"Attractive woman, shorter than me! Where did she go?"

He shrugs. "Wagon left half a bell ago for the city. Wanted to beat the rain. Was a lady on that."

Cursing, I find a fresh mount.

~ | ~

Arriving in the small street that houses the clockwork shop, I spot the same urchin from the other week and toss a copper to watch my horse. I stride into the store then pull up short, remembering that there are many delicate creations and I was not to go barreling into them like a bull at a gate.

The last thing you want is to cause more damage! I cough, hoping someone had heard the door. Muffled voices come from the back room but show no sign of coming closer.

"Hello?" I call.

A harried looking Olaf appears. "Oh! Lady… sorry, Dame al Stauberg. Can I help you?"

"Is your niece here? I intended to bring her back from the palace but she disappeared while I was—ah, Mistress Yulic," I bow to Monique's mother, who steps into the shop. "I was just enquiring."

"Monique is here," Leticia Yulic answers curtly, wringing her hands on her apron. "I've just put her to bed, she needs to rest. Is there a problem?"

"Problem?" *Aside from me almost getting your daughter killed and she's understandably furious about it.* "No, I just wanted to ensure she was alright. I was meant to bring her back but she... left without me." It occurs to me that I, not Monique, had been the one who had departed the stable yard abruptly, with no warning of how long she should wait. "Uh, may I see her?"

Leticia purses her lips. "Come through."

Through the workroom she leads, the scent of paint and freshly carved wood as strong as before, into a tiny kitchen. A table has been shoved to the side to make way for an arrangement of stools that lets Monique sit with her injured ankle elevated.

"Why did you not wait?" I demand, then soften my tone when I see the glare from Leticia. "I was going to bring you home."

My gorgeous woman is pale. Exhaustion wracks her features. "You were busy. I was tired. There was a wagon leaving, so I begged a lift. You didn't need to come chasing after me."

I frown. "I needed to make sure you made it home safely. It's my duty to protect you."

Anger crosses Monique's face. "You may consider your duty discharged. I am back with my family—they will care for me."

My heart drops like a stone. There's no hint of the carefree, teasing Monique, forgiving of my indiscretions and sanguine about our time together. This Monique is cold and sharp.

She keeps speaking. "And while I thank you for the opportunity to paint for the palace, you are not obliged in any way to concern yourself with any ongoing welfare." Her Breyten accent strengthens, the clipped vowels making her sound even harsher.

Stung, I bow. "Forgive me. I wish you a swift recovery." Not knowing what else to do, I exit the shop, ignoring Olaf's half-hearted farewell, snarling at the urchin to get out of my way as I swing into the saddle.

Of course, she's disappointed in you. That's why she was so quiet all the way back to Zivalj. Stupid to think she would want to keep seeing you after you failed so badly. Unreliable in duty, unreliable with lovers.

I can't focus. The city streets pass in a blur until I canter through the gate that opens onto the road up to the palace. The rain starts to fall. Not heavy, like it will through winter, but solid enough to take me straight back into my childhood as I slow the horse to a trot.

"Where is Yatina?" I hear my mother call. "She can't even finish her chores without getting distracted! Now the rain will get all the clothes wet again! Hurry, help me get them in!"

I'd been lying on the barn roof, watching the clouds scud across the sky, fascinated by the shapes and whorls. I'd chased a crow up there after it had stolen a shiny rock I'd been looking at, then stayed when the movement of the clouds had caught my eye. I would incur my mother's wrath if I were caught, I stay hidden while the rain plasters my hair to my face, soaking through my tunic.

Tempting as it is to rush, I don't want my horse to slip, so I raise my hood and slow even more as the rain strengthens. *At least my hair is short these days. Less complicated, just like everything else should be.* The main palace gate rises ahead. *Slow down. Do one thing at a time.* Now isn't the time to think about Monique.

Now I will do my duty as a soldier and serve.

Twelve

Three weeks on the border and I'm relieved my squad remains uninjured despite several clashes with Trevi raiding parties.

"The enemy retreated quickly," I report to Princess Rhea in the headquarters set up in Caelon.

"Opportunists." The princess puts down her quill and rubs her forehead. She looks at Gereon, who sits at a desk beside her, looking equally tired. "That's all these raids seem to be. Thetin isn't committing to a frontal assault; he's just bleeding us. And the rivers are already rising. If they burst their banks, we'll be cut off from supplies. I thought a show of force would make him back down, but now I've over-committed our forces and left the river lands vulnerable."

"Your Highness, if you weren't here the Trevi would have ripped through the farmlands and Caelon might have fallen," I remind. My family's farm is not far from her, and while I haven't been able to see them, my brother had sent a sincere letter expressing his gratitude that the crown had ridden to their defense. He also mentioned that soldiers billeted on the farm were depleting the food stores at a rapid rate and did I know if there was an intention to recompense or resupply farmers?

"I know," Rhea sighs. "But I cannot ask Huon to bear the brunt of the defense when technically this land is Medvajan." She gives her husband a rueful look.

"My mother spares what soldiers she can," Gereon murmurs. "I am sorry it is not more, my dear, but I am her youngest son."

Rhea shakes her head. "She will not leave the southern coasts weak to the Breytens. I understand. I need another solution."

I force myself to stand very straight. "I... I was not successful in asking the dragons for help last time."

"I know," Rhea answers calmly. "But you raised it casually, as you said. It was not a formal request." She taps her fingers. A scribe came in, bowed, left a sheaf of papers on her desk and left. Rhea frowns at the pile. "I need to speak with Kyan, but my presence here is needed. I cannot send Gereon—he is the reason Huon sent soldiers—nor Liam—I rely on him for my chain of command. You are the next most experienced person when it comes to conversing with dragons, so you need to speak with my authority."

My jaw tightens. "My last... dealing wasn't particularly harmonious, your highness."

Rhea waves a hand in dismissal. "By your own account, the artist left the camp alone and without telling anyone."

"I should have been alert and stopped her."

"Be as that may, you contained the situation. It could have been far worse. There is enough uncertainty and apprehension from more conservative elements about our arrangement with the dragons without the death of a young woman sullying our efforts. Hence the artwork, which was your idea in the first place."

I should have just kept my mouth shut. I focus on the portrait behind Rhea's head—it's King Denusake, depicted most regally on a white charger.

"Yatina," Rhea catches my attention. "It was a good idea. That's why I need you. You think on your feet. You lead your squad well. You care about the civilians for which you are responsible."

I'm not up to this!

"You said the artist was due to deliver a painting to one of the dragons in Valesk, yes?"

"Yes, Your Highness." How had Monique been, these last few weeks? Surely her ankle was healed, and she'd been drawing and painting and... what? Dancing? My heart sinks just thinking about it. *Are they struggling? Is she warm enough? I should have sent a winter cloak for her before I left.*

"Yatina!"

I jolt. "Yes, Your Highness!"

"I want you go with them and convey my desire for a meeting with Kyan as soon as possible. Ask…" the princess hesitates. "Ask what the kingdom of Medvaja could offer in exchange for draconic support."

How must she feel, being so responsible for her people? How can I say no? It is my duty.

"It shall be done, your highness."

"Thank you, Yatina." Princess Rhea beckons the scribe who sits on a stool in the corner, ready for whenever the princess needs to dictate. "Draw up the promotional paper for Captain al Stauberg," she orders.

"Your Highness?" I start.

Rhea flashes a grin. "If you are going to speak for me, you need a bit more authority."

I swallow, chest bursting with pride just as my insides clench. "Thank you, Your Highness."

Now, don't mess this up.

~ | ~

There is no point sending a messenger ahead. I ride with minimal escort and we move fast. Anasta, Andrej and Emil. The water below the bridge at Caelon flows high and fast, and we all look forward to one night in the capital to dry off before the final stretch.

I send them ahead to the palace and I enter the city instead. Dusk falls early at this time of year, so many shutters are already fastened when I reach the shop. No urchin in sight, I hitch my horse to a railing and glare at the darkening street, mentally daring thieves to try their luck. I am not in the mood.

I knock loudly, pulling my cloak tight against the drizzle. When there's no answer, I bang again.

"*Ja,* who is there?" Olaf's reedy voice sounds on the other side. "The shop is closed, please to come back in the morning, *ja?*"

"Master Yulic, it's Yatina al Stauberg, from the palace," I call.

"May I come in? I need to speak to Monique." I pray she hasn't left for Valesk early.

A pause while the only sound is my horse shaking its head, sending water droplets spraying. Then a bolt is drawn and the door swings inwards a crack. Olaf looks worried.

"Of course. Come in out of the wet." He doesn't sound anywhere as enthusiastic as he did the first few times I'd been here, but I try to ignore it. He probably blames me for almost getting Monique killed, too.

"Have, uh, people been buying the clockwork?" I ask in an attempt to extend a truce.

He shoots me a surprised look. "*Ja*, some. Lords and ladies, but also merchants. We must be thankful." He doesn't say to whom.

We enter the workroom. My cloak drips on the floorboards as I behold Monique rolling a great piece of canvas to fit into a long wooden tube. I catch a glimpse of bright colors—reds and blues and dramatic black.

"Dame al Stauberg, Lead Spear of the royal guard."

Is she mocking me? I clear my throat.

"It's captain now, actually." *Do you think that will impress her?*

As if to prove me right, Monique raises her eyebrows. "Congratulations, captain." We stare at each other.

"Your ankle, is it healed?" I enquire stiffly, repressing the urge to pick up the other woman and bury my face in those beautiful black waves.

Monique brandishes the limb in question. "Mostly. It's still a little sore, but I can walk. Until I stupidly fall again."

"Uh, good." Now it sounds like I've said 'good' to her falling. *I'm an idiot.*

We stare at each other. Shame swells within me. This is the one person I think I wouldn't have got bored of, wouldn't want to leave, but she deserves someone better. Someone thoughtful, and careful, and faithful.

I swallow. "I'm to accompany you to Valesk. Not for protection!" I add as Monique bristles. "The princess has asked me to request an urgent meeting with Kyan."

Monique frowns, concerned. "We've not had much news. Do things not go well in the north?"

"Well enough," I hedge, "but the princess is exploring options."

Monique considers this. "Well, you're just in time. I was going to leave tomorrow. I'm trying to make sure everything is wrapped in oilskin, so it's well protected." She runs her eyes up and down me, making me feel exposed despite the layers I wear. "Do you want to come and dry off by the fire?"

I shake my head, wishing I could stay but knowing I need to leave her in peace. "I'd better get to the palace. What bell will you leave by?"

"Second, if I can get the cart loaded. You can meet me by the northern gate."

I want to offer to be there and help load, but don't.

"I will see you then."

~ | ~

The rain holds off as we ride along the muddy road to Valesk. Monique's small flatbed, pulled by a stolid carthorse, keeps the pace of the party slow. I toss a thick cloak at Monique when the breeze picks up.

"What's this?" Monique asks, perplexed.

"A cloak. Wear it. Yours is too thin."

Monique frowns, but doesn't argue.

As we near the village, I send the others ahead and hang back to ride beside the cart.

I look meaningfully at Monique several times before she finally sighs. "I don't need you to look after me."

This is deeper than just the cloak, or riding at the slower pace of the carthorse. I had a lot of time to think last night, when I should have been sleeping. I can't bear to not try again.

"Has is occurred to you," I ask carefully, "that I care what happens to you."

"I won't be an obligation."

I look up at the gray sky, considering. "What part of this makes you think I feel obliged to you?"

"I know how you feel about duty! And I know you get tired of people once you sleep with them! I didn't want you feeling like you have to stick around when you want to move on."

I twist the reins in my hands. My bay snorts. "I didn't tire of you." *But you told her you would. That it's inevitable.*

"But you would have. You made that very clear." She takes a deep breath and out pours a torrent of words that she has clearly ruminated on. "I thought I was fine to enjoy what we had. Then after that night... I knew I had to pull back because I couldn't let myself want more. It's why I pushed you towards the herder. I wanted to let you know I wouldn't cling on, wouldn't keep you trapped. Then I stupidly injured myself and I knew you would be too honorable to leave until you felt you had 'fixed' things. You would have stayed and grown to resent me."

Dumbfounded, I stare sidelong at Monique, too astonished to look at her directly. "You thought I'd resent you?"

"Wouldn't you? That day you said the 'feelings won't last. They never do'. How does that fit when you feel honor-bound to support the poor dancer and her family?"

The village comes into sight. Monique clucks her tongue and shakes the reins to hurry the carthorse, who ignores her with remarkable aplomb. My forehead creases as I think about what she's said. Yes, I feel obliged to help the Yulic family because I'd caused them to suffer a loss of income by allowing Monique to get injured! But... I never saw Monique as a burden. *Would you have, though?*

"I just wanted to help," I say quietly. "I thought we might have a chance together, without getting tired of each other. Or... me getting tired of you, since that's the real problem. But the way I'm drawn to you is unlike anything—"

Then a dragon flies over and interrupts our conversation.

~ | ~

The horses almost lose their minds, so it is with great effort and much cursing we bring them to the side of the road and hitch them to a tree. We trudge up the nearby hill where the dragons crouch patiently. Kamelya's vivid red scales, Dorukhan's dark bulk, and Kyan's shimmering emerald brighten the bald ground amidst the sparse trees. Half a year ago, I never would have envisioned myself approaching three adult dragons with little more than irritation.

"We thought it best not to descend upon the village," Kyan says, bowing his head politely as we reach the summit.

I was going to use the horn, I think sardonically, but manage to keep the comment quiet. They may be still angry at the injury I'd caused to the young dragon, and I owe it to my princess to be as courteous as possible in the hope this endeavor will succeed.

"We appreciate that," I answer before Monique can speak. "Princess Rhea and Prince Gereon send their greetings and good wishes. They hope you are in good health and did not have an arduous journey here." Never mind my own journey had been waterlogged and cold. Even now, the threat of rain hovers in the near distance.

"I hope dear Rhea and Gereon are well," Kyan replies. "I had hoped they would be here also, now that their marriage ceremony has taken place." His voice is tinged with disappointment.

"They would be here if they could," I apologize. "War is brewing on our northern border with Trevault, and it is their duty to lead our soldiers and protect the farmers and merchants who live there."

A shuffle as Kamelya and Dorukhan look at each other, but they say nothing.

"I know how seriously Princess Rhea takes her duty to her people." Kyan inclines his head.

It takes everything in me not to give out a nervous laugh. I carry on. "But she would value a meeting with you. In fact, she sent me here to beg such a thing of you."

Kyan raises an eye ridge. "She wishes me to go to her?"

"Just to speak." I spread my hands wide. "It would be easier if we had some means of conveying messages across distance, but she urgently begs a meeting of you, and she cannot leave her soldiers easily, especially because the rivers may flood soon and she will be cut off."

Kyan settles back on his haunches, considering. He doesn't look at Kamelya or Dorukhan, who shift restlessly.

"Her predicament is worse than I realized," Kyan responds slowly. "A meeting I can grant her, though I suspect I know what she will ask." He flicks a glance at Kamelya then, who looks back boldly.

"The council won't approve," she warns.

Kyan nodded. "I know. But perhaps we can change enough of their minds. I have an idea that might help."

Thirteen

"You should have stayed," I mutter for the tenth time as Monique shivers in my arms, the mountain air freezing us both.

Not that she can hear me as the wind is as loud as it is cold, rushing in our eyes as the flap, flap of Kamelya's wings beat a steady pace and we cross peaks I've had never seen before, let alone from the sky.

We are *flying*. It's the most exhilarating thing I've ever done and I'm terrified, but so very alive. Straddling Kamelya's neck just ahead of her powerful shoulders, I thank a lifetime of horse-riding that give my thighs the strength to grip as I hold onto Monique tightly, who in turn grips the ridges that flare down from the red dragon's crest.

"Not long now!" Kamelya calls back, wingbeats unfaltering.

Hold on a little longer, I urge Monique, so grateful to have her in my arms but wishing again that it was only me who was flying into danger. Who knows how the other dragons might receive us? While Anasta, tough, stoic Anasta, flies with Kyan to Caelon, Monique and I are headed in the opposite direction, with Dorukhan carrying the tightly wrapped bundle of Monique's paintings to show to their clan.

"A cultural exchange," Kyan had proclaimed. "It will help the others see that you are intelligent beings worthy of our alliance."

Assuming they don't just eat us. My thoughts are not particularly diplomatic right now, focused as I am on not falling off, not freezing, and not letting go of Monique. Besides, I'm no ambassador!

My stomach lurches as Kamelya drops into a long, shallow dive. We soar along the path of a furious, rushing river, canyon walls rising either side in precarious proximity, until we burst out over a waterfall into the wide space beyond. I feel Monique gasp. A plateau lays like a giant shelf, abutted on three steep sides by mountainsides that appear to be riddled with caves. The western side falls away to the sea below, glittering like diamond in the late afternoon sun. The river curls back and forth across the plateau like a basking snake, then plummets down the cliff and vanishes from my sight. I wonder if there is land below that I can't see, or if the gushing snowmelt falls straight into the ocean.

Kamelya banks, aiming for a medium-sized opening on the northern side. As we get closer, other dragons call out greetings in their own tongue, either from ledges or in the air as they beat past, necks craning at the strange passengers the red dragon bears.

A final swoop, and we alight.

"We made it!" Kamelya declares cheerfully. "Can you get down without falling?" She lowers her neck as close to the ground as she can manage. I slide off and stagger, then recover enough to catch Monique, wondering if my own nose and cheeks are bright red with cold.

"I might crack in half from being frozen, but that…" I shake my head in awe. "I don't know what to say." The feeling of flying still fills my chest. "If I die tomorrow, I can say I had the privilege of flying on a dragon." I feel humbled. It is nothing like riding a horse, where you steer and control. I'd had to trust that Kamelya would deliver us without incident, and here we are.

The red dragon cocks her head and draws a half smile, several teeth peeking over her lip.

"Thank you for getting us here safely." Monique's teeth chatter as she looks about. "Does Dorukhan still have the paintings?" The black dragon had split off once we reached the plateau but I'd been too busy taking in the sights to notice where he'd gone.

"He's taking them to the council cave. I'll join him momentarily. I just thought it would be better if I stashed you two here for now. Eat something, warm up—let us prepare the others before we frighten them with your presence." She winks. "Let me show you my weyr."

We follow her away from the ledge and into the cave. Kamelya waves a claw and pale blue lights wink into existence. Crystals embedded into the ceiling of the rock, illuminating the—what did she call it? The weyr.

For cave is entirely the wrong word. Not a basic cleft in the rock, not rough, nor damp, not dark. This space is shaped and smooth, with carved runes and patterns along the many shelves and recesses that seemed molded from the cave wall itself.

"This… is incredible," Monique breathes. She looks at me and gestures. "Are you seeing this?"

Bemused, Kamelya peers around in confusion. "Seeing what?"

"You have… decorations, and shelves, and lights!" I blurt. "Are those books?" Great tomes with thick leather covers, each half my height, clustered on high stone shelves. Colorful weavings and fused wood and bone sculptures hang from little outcrops that act as hooks. Kamelya flicks another claw and small sparks light sticks of incense fitted into holders on either side of the space, the wafting smoke infusing the air with an earthy fragrance.

"Of course," the dragon replies, bemused. "I do study. The weaving was a gift from my mother. I traded some labor for the bonedancer sculptures, but I am getting better at bespelling light crystals—I thought we established that I like art."

Monique raises her eyebrows at me. "We did not realize you had… such good taste. I hope my paintings can live up to it." She is sincere, I know. I'm no expert on art—I prefer to look at either weaponry or a pretty face—but the way Monique rotates slowly and takes in the space makes me suspect that Kamelya has done well. Even the glowing crystals are placed strategically to highlight the decorations.

"And this is your personal… weyr?" There is a large wooden tree trunk, carved and smooth to form an odd shaped table in the center of the cave. Someone Dorukhan's size would find it a squeeze but at least three dragons would be able to fit around it. What did they use it for? Meals? Study? Games?

"It is." Kamelya's voice is tinged with pride. "It's small, but I shaped it myself when I came into possession. I've a sleep nook," she points to a deep ledge cut into the side wall, adorned with huge animal skins, "and fresh water runs through the back. You can clean up if you want and rest, though I'll have to find something for you to climb onto to get up there."

"It certainly doesn't seem small to me," I offer. The dragon laughs. *I hope this means she's no longer angry about me hurting the youngling.*

"No. I suppose not." She ends up using some of the books to create a small staircase for Monique and me to reach the sleep ledge and pulls down some strips of dried meat from a jar. "Don't tell Kyan I used the books, he'll kill me."

"We won't breathe a word," Monique promises, looking much more alive now we have eaten and refreshed ourselves. While the water that runs along the channel at the back of the weyr isn't by any means large enough for a dragon to bathe in, it's more than adequate for two humans to strip off and clean up. The air deeper in the cave isn't as chill as outside, but we don't linger, so I only have the chance to steal a handful of glances at Monique as we bathe.

"The sun is setting." Kamelya looks at the shadows streaming across the outside ledge. "Stay here, stay warm, while I attend the council meeting. Sleep if you like. I expect the councilors will want to see you tomorrow, but I will tell you ⟨…⟩ I return."

⟨…⟩e is going to be… angry at you, are they? Or us, for ⟨…⟩ I want to know what the dangers of being here ⟨…⟩

⟨…⟩ on Kyan's word. He may be one of ⟨…⟩ he is a master of spell work and ⟨…⟩other you."

⟨…⟩ne would bother her, but accept ⟨…⟩d in farewell as the red dragon ⟨…⟩ with a sharp beat of wings.

~ | ~

"Are you tired?" I ask Monique, turning back into the cave. *It's a weyr. Stop calling it a cave in case you insult someone.*

Monique gives a faint smile from where she sits on one of the book steps. "Exhausted. And a bit overwhelmed. I think I will sleep. You?"

My instincts scream that I should stand guard, but if Kamelya is wrong and another dragon did choose to invade the space, what could I actually do? It's hard to admit to myself, but sleep is the most sensible thing I can do right now.

"I'll rest too. I'll just use the… I suppose it's a privy." Kamelya had pointed out the hidden alcove past the water channel, also adorned with smoldering incense. A woven curtain falls across the opening, giving privacy, but also giving me something to hold onto as I brave the dragon sized latrine. I throw in scented ash afterwards as I'd been instructed and wash my hands, then shuck off my boots and climb up the book staircase to find Monique already curled up on a thick bear skin, cloaks layered over her.

I hesitate, then wrap my own cloak around my shoulders and sit on a soft wolf pelt nearby. I gaze at Monique's lovely face, her eyes closed. My heart aches and I consider once again the bravery of this woman, her quiet strength and beauty.

Without opening her yes, Monique murmurs, "We'll be warmer if you sleep next to me."

"I… didn't want to disturb you." The truth is I don't know if I can bear to be so close without touching her, and touching will set off a series of stupid actions that I may regret. If Monique doesn't want me, I won't be that person, no matt how fiercely my body yearns.

Three weeks on the border and I'd avoided sex comp' My excuse was that I'd needed to focus, to lead my squ and stay alert for Trevi soldiers attempting sneak attack truth is there had been plenty of opportunities. A f lieutenant from a Huon patrol squad. A moon-eyed daughter where we'd camped in the fields. Not to mention the sharp and savvy prostitutes in Caelon, who were one of the few groups benefitting from the increased military presence.

But shame and regret colored my thoughts every time the possibility had arisen. I didn't want to just scratch the itch, like I'd always done before. I want Monique—I crave her in a way that is far more than just physical.

"Well?" the object of my desire rolls over and opens her eyes. "Are you going to—? Oh, Yatina." Monique takes one look at my face and reaches for me. I hold very still, her cold hand on my too hot face, a soothing balm for the fire that rages within.

"I need you," I say haltingly. "I want to be a better person when I am with you." *Am I even making sense?*

Monique cups my cheek. "You are a good person already. You are dutiful, honorable, courageous."

"I'm not!" I draw in a deep breath. "I mean, I'm not terrible. But when I'm with you I want to be better. I feel... better, with you. It's not duty, you're not an obligation." She winces at the word. "I want more than just to have you in bed—I want to see you happy and prospering. I know I haven't done the best by you, but I want to try."

Monique withdraws her hand, then replaces it, rubbing her thumb gently on my face. "I'm scared of getting hurt," she admits. "I told you we should just enjoy the moments but... when I start to care for someone, it's hard for me to not want more."

"Were you just trying to push me away then?" I shake my head. "I thought you were angry at me for letting you get hurt. I never thought of you as a burden."

She looks down. "I *was* a burden, Yatina. You had already done so much, giving me the opportunity to support my family in a different way, and I almost got a young dragon killed. Then you had to carry me, then..." She meets my eyes. "I knew you well enough by then to know you'd keep looking after me because you felt obliged to. I want you to be with me because you want to, not out of a sense of duty."

"I do want you," I avow, capturing Monique's hand with my own. "My eye may stray, temptation will cross my path, but I don't think I could get bored with you." I kiss her palm. "I actually thought you were trying to tell me that was a possibility. That we might take other lovers now and then but still be together.

She draws a sharp breath. "Other lovers are fine, as long as you tell me, and come back to me out of desire, not duty."

I rise up on my knees and pull Monique close. "Oh, I desire you." My lips press to hers fervently, seeking and giving assurance that there is no duty, only want.

I pull back enough to remove our cloaks and lay them over the skins. Hands trembling, I tug off my thick woolen tunic and the quilted shirt that lies beneath. I steal kiss after kiss as Monique fumbles with her own laces, running my mouth and teeth along the now exposed shoulders and collarbone.

"I don't care how cold is," I mutter, "I need to touch you."

"Oh, yes," Monique answers breathlessly, freeing herself of her dress and standing to slide out of her leggings. I gaze up, a supplicant worshiping my goddess. Caressing her slim, strong thighs, I move forward on my knees and kiss her, right at her center, reveling in the shudder it causes.

"Another night I will explore you slowly," I promise. "And many nights after that. But tonight I need you."

"Take me," Monique begs, then gasps as my tongue cleaves her, her back arching with ardor.

Fourteen

Fingers grasping thighs and ass, I moan in relief and joy as I taste Monique's sweetness. Her heavenly scent washes over me, almost driving me to a frenzy. I plunge my tongue in and along every honeyed fold, reveling in her shudders and cries. Gripping even tighter when I feel knees begin to buckle, I steady her as I kiss and lave and bury my face in her.

She cries out and almost collapses. I guide her to the floor, gentle now.

"Kiss me," Monique implores, then moans as I comply and she tastes her own creaminess on my mouth. Then, breathlessly, as her hands creep down to my ass, "Why are you still wearing trousers?"

I grin, wriggling out of them as fast as I can. I straddle Monique's leg and kiss her again, rocking myself to pleasure. Monique teases my breasts as I ride her, strumming my nipples to hard pebbles, then licking and sucking them as I climax, so taut with need my release can't come soon enough.

I fold forward onto Monique, and we exchange a smile, the flurry of lovemaking morphing swiftly from simple joy to something deeper. Her eyes are as dark and as deep as the ocean, and I cannot help but kiss her ever so tenderly.

"You are… I don't even have the words for what you are." It grips my chest. "Magnificent. Wonderful. Incredible." And suddenly I'm not afraid anymore. Not afraid of getting bored, that the passion would fade. The way I am drawn to Monique isn't to scratch that itch, to chase a fresh distraction. She is as exciting as she is comforting. I feel both thrilled and safe with her.

Monique kisses me. "*We* are wonderful."

We lie content in our warmth under the cloak I pull over us. "We should get dressed," Monique sighs.

I grumble, but sit up and began reaching for our clothes. A shadow in the main cave brings my attention up fast, and I leap to my feet. Monique shrieks at the cold influx of air as the cloak shifts.

"It's just me!" Kamelya calls cheerily. "Oh!" Her slit-pupiled eyes go wide. "Why are you not wearing anything?" she enquires. "Surely it's far too cold for humans… oh!" She notices Monique and sniffs the air, then chuckles. "You decided to warm up another way."

I frown and cast about for my shirt.

"We're so sorry," Monique blurts, a dark flush creeping over her honeyed skin.

"We are?" I stuff my head into the shirt.

"Yatina! It's her home—her bed!"

"Oh." When she puts it like that, I feel crass.

Kamelya slinks closer, crouching so her head rests on the edge of the sleeping nook. "I don't mind," she tells Monique. "You both know I'm curious about how humans copulate. If I didn't think it would embarrass you both, I'd use it as an example to the council of how humans aren't just animals, mating for offspring."

I swing around, abandoning my trousers. "Don't you dare!"

Kamelya laughs. "I won't." Her eyes flick over Monique, who still sits with the cloak clutched over her breasts, shoulders bare. My lover draws in a sharp breath.

"You *are* very curious, aren't you?" I say to Kamelya, then kneel beside Monique and kiss her cheek. "And so were you." I run my fingers through her hair. "I saw you together when we were in the mountains."

"You saw?"

I give a half smile. "You were beautiful." I hesitate. "It made me realize that I could not tire of someone so adventurous. So inspiring." My gaze slides back to Kamelya. "And I could not resent someone who also finds you so captivating."

The dragon closes her eyes in acknowledgment. "It is true."

Monique's breath hitches again and her pupils dilate in the crystal light. "So you aren't worried that it's not 'normal'? Or think me shameful for not staying faithful?"

I give a slow smile, then kiss her deliberately. "Didn't we just declare that desire trumps duty for us? I desire to see you happy. And I can hardly shame you for a lack of fidelity when it is not something I can achieve myself." I look at Kamelya. "As for normal—we are more alike than different, are we not?"

Kamelya leans close, sniffing both of us. Her own scent was that one I'd identified that first meeting—large and warm, not reptilian at all, strong without being overpowering. I'm turned on, not so much for myself, but for the effect she is having on Monique. "I desire you," I whisper, "and so does she."

"Very much so," the dragon murmurs.

Breathing faster, Monique lets the cloak slip to her lap, revealing herself. "I want you both," she breathes.

Kamelya bends her head right down and rasps her tongue gently over Monique's soft skin. Monique gives a little cry—shock and pleasure, I know the sound well.

"Lie back," I whisper, cradling my lover as the dragon traces her tongue between Monique's breasts, across her nipples, down each arm. I pull the cloak away and hold Monique's hands tightly, watching as Kamelya trails clawtips down each leg, our combine effort forcing her to submit to the pleasure.

"Taste her," I encourage, my own mouth watering. I squeeze my thighs as the sight of Monique melting brings the heat. Would I want a dragon to nuzzle me there? I'm not entirely certain, but the sight of Monique getting licked by that surprisingly dexterous tongue arouses me hugely. "You're beautiful," I declare, kissing Monique as Kamelya's tongue sweeps in. A guttural growl brings a shriek of pleasure to my gorgeous creature, and I free one hand to touch myself. Instantly slippery, I gasp and press one of Monique's hands to my breast.

"On me," Monique gasps. "Please, I need you on my face."

I oblige, kneeling across her, reveling in the sight of her taut naked form before me.

Her warm mouth sets upon me, no teasing or delay, and a moan escapes me. Rocking into bliss on her hungry mouth, I feel none of the stress that usually comes with someone else pleasuring me, because I can see very plainly how well Kamelya is looking after my lover.

The dragon tongue slides in and out from between her legs. It's lewd and so sexy that I grasp her ankles and raise them, giving Kamelya better access. The dragon reaches forward and places delicate claws on my thighs. I shiver at the danger but continue to grind until I come hard, sliding off and kissing Monique as Kamelya penetrates her again and again, great, vibrating growls sending her back arching again and again.

"Oh…" Monique closes her eyes in bliss as the dragon finally relents. I pull her into my arms and hold her tight.

"Beautiful," I whisper, kissing the dark hair that sweat has curled into ringlets. "You are utterly beautiful." I inhale deeply, savoring the scent, sex mixed with dragon.

Monique gives a lazy smile, eyes still closed. "But how do we pleasure you, Kamelya?" she lilts.

"Mmm." The red dragon crawls into the sleep nook, careful to wrap around us. "You could touch my wings gently…" She splays one over us, darkening the space and creating an even more intimate feel. Monique reaches up and trails her fingers down the fragile span between the wingbones, and is rewarded with a sharp intake of air.

"Like this?"

"Yes," Kamelya growls, and despite the situation I tense. Then I reach out hesitantly myself and marvel at the paper thin softness—the light of the roof crystals shining dimly through the webbed membrane.

Monique sighs. Knowing what I do of her, it's entirely possible the pleasure she is receiving through her palms and fingertips could very well match the low rumbles of enjoyment from the dragon. I shake my head in awe. How she derives gratification through her hands, her mouth, through almost anywhere in her body, is beyond me! But I love it. I love her.

Emboldened, I reach further along the wing, stroking the skin where it molds itself onto delicate bones, running my hand down the bones themselves.

Kamelya shifts and rolls half onto her back, exposing her underside, breathing heavily.

"Where else should I touch you?" Monique murmurs.

"Down." The long tail encircling us twitches. Between the dragons legs a slit is visible, moisture gleaming on the thin lips. Monique slides down on her knees and gently touches her hand to the top of the slit.

Kamelya groans. Monique teases, seductive and sultry as the dragon curls her neck to watch. I watch too, entranced, but continued to stroke Kamelya's wings as Monique uses her whole palm in the same way she might have used two fingers on a human woman. Deliberate but light, she circles, spreading the gleaming wetness as the slit slowly swells and Kamelya's tail beats an increasing tempo on the rock wall.

The dragon's eyes seem to glow—her wings twitch away then return to me. I waver.

"Don't stop, please," Kamelya twitches again involuntarily. "Be firmer, they won't break."

Unsure, I grasp the top wingbone and hold it out as I trace and trail back and forth. Kamelya shudders. Her tail beats even faster. My nails are no claws, but I drag them carefully down the membrane, inhaling that deep warm scent. It has a tart edge now, and I find myself leaning closer to breathe it in. Bizarrely, I want to taste—she smells like rich, ripe cherries and I can't help but brush the tip of my tongue along one wing.

A shock like the static from woolen blankets on a dry night zings through me, hardening my nipples and causing me to jerk in shock. I lick again, then whimper out loud at the lightning coursing through my veins. I cannot think straight. Is this how Monique feels when she climaxes with her mouth?

Still holding Kamelya's wing, I crane my neck to look at Monique, who swirls and caresses along the dragon's slit. Her hand teases as she dips lower. Kamelya moans, Monique pants, both clearly close.

"Inside?" Monique demands to know, eyes flashing.

"Please!"

The dragon groans as Monique pushes her whole hand in with a shuddering cry. My jaw drops. Kamelya roars and undulates, a beautiful wave of movement full of suppressed thrashing. As Monique withdraws and strokes her way free, her face full of bliss, the dragon emits little growls and twitches.

"Come up here," she commands.

Monique crawls up to join me at Kamelya's chest. To my astonishment, the dragon's quim closes up until it is barely discernable as overlapping scales, then Kamelya resettles herself on her belly, tail encircling us.

Monique looks at me, a bashful smile on her face. "Was that good?" She glances at the dragon, whose head tucks in to blink sleepily. "For both of you?"

Kamelya yawns hugely. "Most definitely. It's not often I find a lover capable of paying attention to small details." She grins, her teeth a fearsome display.

Monique is still watching me. I give her a wry smile and a low whistle. "I didn't think I could get bored before, now I know no one will ever compare to you." I kiss her sincerely. "You are truly incredible, and I'm privileged to call you my lover." I nod to the dragon, blushing a little. "Thank you, Kamelya."

Kamelya nudges me gently with her snout. "As long as you enjoy yourself too, brave dame."

"I did," I admit. "I'd be keen to do it again, actually." I shrug apologetically. "A long way from thinking you were just a winged lizard."

Kamelya chortles. Monique frowns as she rests her head against my chest. She locates one of our cloaks by her feet and tugs it up. "You called her a winged lizard? That's horribly rude."

"I didn't call her that!"

The dragon interjects with another enormous yawn. "I must admit, for a furless bear you've impressed me."

I make an obscene gesture.

"Don't argue, I'm sleepy," Monique complains, sliding down. "I like you both, so please be nice to each other." She closes her eyes.

I gaze at her affectionately, then wink at the dragon. "I can be nice. Very nice."

Kamelya nudges me again, then settles her head on the wolf skin pelt. "I think I can manage that too." Her lips curl up and her teeth peek out. "And tomorrow we'll convince the council that humans are worth being friends with."

A profound sense of pride rolls through me. It might not be straight away, but I will be part of the effort that forges an alliance with dragons. I look down at Monique, now asleep in my arms.

"Thank you," I say, quietly and sincerely.